MYSTERY IN THE HILL

by

Aaron Qualio

DORRANCE
PUBLISHING CO
EST. 1920
PITTSBURGH, PENNSYLVANIA 15238

Dorrance Publishing Co
585 Alpha Drive, Suite 103
Pittsburgh, PA 15238
Visit our website at *www.dorrancebookstore.com*

ISBN: 978-1-6491-3112-6
eISBN 978-1-6491-3619-0

MYSTERY IN THE HILL

Chapter One

It was the last period of the school day on a Friday in mid-May at Ash-belle High School, and the seniors in Mr. Winters's U.S. History class were pretty much checked out just like seniors all over the country were this close to graduation—"senioritis" they called it. Joel Winters, as did all the other teachers, tried his best to keep seniors interested this last month of school, and he felt that what he was teaching today just might do the trick.

"Thanks to the many recently declassified documents from World War II, we're now aware of all sorts of previously unknown things that went on in this country during that time," said Winters. "For example, we know that the United States government secretly paid for and built tunnels under some factories in America that were producing certain wartime products in case an attack occurred on U.S. soil. The thought process was that if the enemy attacked, the workers could get out safely and secretly even if their factory was bombed."

"Mr. Winters, didn't the Ashbelle Company produce bombs during World War II?" asked Andrew Quimby. "Is it possible there are tunnels like that here?"

"Yes they did," Winters replied, "but records show that the factories where these tunnels were built were mainly on the coasts, as that's where the enemy was most likely to bomb. There are a few examples of factories in the center of the country where tunnels were built, but those were factories that were producing much, much more material than Ashbelle. The U.S. government must not have thought that Ashbelle, and other companies doing relatively the same amount of production as they were, would've been a likely target had bombings occurred, especially this far from the coasts. Okay class, that's the bell. Have a nice weekend. Next time we'll discuss more things that were recently declassified from the World War II era."

Andrew decided to hang back as the other students left the classroom and came up to Winters's desk after the rest of the students had filed out. "I know you said there are no records and that it's unlikely, but it'd be so cool if those tunnels existed here."

"It would be, Andrew, but I just can't believe that in a town this size, that could've happened without someone knowing about it or finding any tunnels after all these years," replied Winters. "Plus, why not have any records about it? That stuff is all declassified now, so we'd know about it if there were."

"Yeah, makes sense. Just would be cool is all…Have a good one," said Andrew as he turned and walked out in to the hallway.

As Andrew was heading to his locker, he saw Chris Kopp, one of his best friends, heading out.

"What's up, dude?" said Andrew.

"Hey buddy, you still coming over?" replied Chris.

"Yeah, just let me throw some of this crap in my locker and then I'll be there in about fifteen."

"Cool, I look forward to kicking your ass again today," said Chris before he disappeared around the corner.

Andrew just laughed and shook his head. Chris and Andrew had grown up living across the street from one another. When they were little kids, they would play together almost every day—everything from football in the alley behind Andrew's house to king of the mountain on the gigantic snow banks that the Village plows would create in winter on the island between their two streets. Like many kids in the Village, they had also gone to school together since Kindergarten.

Ashbelle was a small village of approximately two thousand residents near Lake Michigan on Wisconsin's east coast. Wisconsin was full of towns like these, but Ashbelle was unique. The Ashbelle Company was a family-owned business for generations and was famous for its high-end electrical fixtures and components, but they were also known for the Village that bore their name.

The Ashbelle family, who still ran it, felt it was their personal responsibility to keep the Village beautiful, safe, and prosperous, and used their influence and money to keep it that way; everything was planned and regulated, which most of the residents didn't mind as it kept Ashbelle as a great place to live, work, and raise a family.

Andrew pulled up to Chris's house and parked. Before he could even say anything, Chris shouted to him from the driveway, "Let's go, this is going to be like the tenth game in a row of HORSE that I beat you at."

"We'll see about that," said Andrew.

Chris was about five foot ten inches with brown hair and brown eyes, and although he was relatively small in frame, he was a good all-around athlete. He had even been named an all-conference wide receiver their senior year of football. Besides that, and probably how he'd describe himself, he was definitely a ladies' man. Chris had several girlfriends, but he was smooth enough where he didn't even have to keep it a secret; the girls knew about each other, but he could make each one feel special enough when he was with them that they thought the others weren't a threat. Andrew attributed Chris's "game" with the ladies somewhat due to the fact that he had been raised by his mom and older sister and therefore knew how girls operated, what they wanted to hear, and so forth. Chris's dad had passed away of a massive heart attack when Chris was only three years old. Apparently he was a great guy from what Andrew had heard.

Andrew was about six feet tall, brown hair, blue eyes, a pretty good student, captain of the football team, and was built more like a linebacker. Andrew was rare in the fact that neither of his parents worked for the Ashbelle Company. In addition to the factory, the Ashbelle Company owned hotels, restaurants, golf courses, shopping areas, and even a sporting club in the Village, so many people in the Village worked for them in some respect.

After Chris had sunk a trick shot from behind the backboard, Andrew said, "Wouldn't it be cool if there were tunnels under Ashbelle like the ones Winters was talking about today?"

"Yeah, I guess, but you heard Winters, there's no way," replied Chris.

Andrew had just attempted the trick shot Chris had just made and missed. "Up yours, you're crushing me. That makes it HORS to HO, right? Why do I even play this with you?"

"I always kill you at this game," replied Chris with a smirk on his face.

"I know. I'm just saying, it'd be awesome if there were tunnels," replied Andrew as he watched Chris drill a three-pointer from the top of the key.

"Boom, that there will probably end it," said Chris while holding his follow-through hand up in the air for effect.

"Damn, you know I'm more of rebounder and fouler than a shooter!" said Andrew as he clanged his three-point attempt off the rim. "Game over. Let's get something to eat."

"Sounds good, let's go see if Trev and Tanner want to make a run," said Chris.

◄o►

As Chris and Andrew walked right in to Tanner's house, they heard Tanner yell, "You cheating son of a bitch!" as Trev just sat there laughing with his hands up in the air. "How do you possibly keep breaking all my tackles?"

"Hey man, don't blame me. The game made Bo Jackson amazing," replied Trev, still laughing as he widened his lead in Tecmo Bowl.

That's another thing about small towns: No one locks their doors—at least during daytime when they're home—and people walk in with a familiarity that, at times, borders on rudeness. But that's how it was, so if you locked your doors or minded kids walking in to your house, you were the one with the problem.

Trev Miles and Tanner Price, also seniors at Ashbelle High, had grown up with Chris and Andrew.

In a town the size of Ashbelle, you have some of the closest friends you can imagine. For basically fifteen years, you see each other pretty much every day. You are in school together, on teams together, go to church together, get in trouble together, and go through life's ups and downs together. You get to know each other's parents, siblings, and pets. You may not always get along, but you know these people have your back and want what's best for you. It's just something that a big town or city can't provide.

Trev was about six foot five inches tall with blond hair and blue eyes. He was good with the ladies and was a solid all-around athlete. He was the quarterback on the football team, a solid player on the golf team, and a pitcher and outfielder on the baseball team. Where Trev really shined, though, was basketball. Obviously his height helped him be a success, but he was also a good three-point shooter, which forced the big trees guarding him to come out to the perimeter, giving him the option of sliding right past them to the hoop. Trev enjoyed basketball, but had recently told the guys that he was kind of getting sick of it. He'd say that his whole life was basketball, basketball, basketball, and now that he was graduating, he didn't think he wanted to play Division II or III ball like most people in town expected him to. Trev also came from a family that had been in Ashbelle for generations. His dad and uncles had been great athletes back in the sixties and seventies, and that added some pressure and also kept Trev playing sports he didn't care for. In particular, Trev and the football coach never quite saw eye to eye and had gotten in to some verbal spats a time or two. Trev had wanted to quit, but figured that wouldn't have gone over well at home.

Andrew and the guys had fortunately been successful at keeping him playing as his height and athleticism made him a solid quarterback.

Tanner was about six foot one inch with blond hair and brown eyes. He was also a solid athlete: pitcher, strong safety, forward in basketball, and Chris's doubles partner on the tennis team. Tanner came from a family of three boys; his parents had been divorced since he'd moved to the Village in second grade, and Andrew felt badly for his mother for how hard she worked at keeping them all in line while still attending nearly every sporting event. She yelled at the boys a bit, but Andrew realized as he had gotten older that that was the only way to get them to listen.

"Boys, who wants to make a food run?" asked Chris.

"I do," replied both Trev and Tanner at the same time.

"T Bell?" asked Trev.

"Oh yeah, a couple dozen soft shells for sure," replied Chris.

"Tanner, why do you look so pissed, man?" asked Andrew.

"Because Trev won't pick any other team in Tecmo Bowl than the Raiders and Bo Jackson is unstoppable," replied Tanner.

"Hey man, it sucks to suck," replied Trev.

"Whatever, jackasses, let's roll," said Chris as the boys headed out the front door to pile in to Andrew's Chevy Blazer. The rule was that the first one to the car got shotgun, and throwing elbows and grabbing were allowed and encouraged. Tanner managed to get to the car first this time as Chris and Trev were locked in some kind of wrestling move.

"Shotgun!" yelled Tanner.

"Damn!" said Chris. "Next time it's mine."

The color of Andrew's Chevy Blazer had always been a good laugh at Andrew's expense. He honestly, 100 percent, swore that it was brown; he wasn't color blind or anything, just had a blind spot in this case.

"Andrew, do you really still think this thing is brown?" asked Tanner.

"Absolutely," replied Andrew.

"Dude, this thing is black as night," said Chris as they all had a good laugh.

"Hey, how are we going to get some beer tonight?" Tanner asked as they began to drive.

They all looked at Andrew, as he was the one among them who had the most facial hair, which wasn't much—a small goatee, if anything. Although it wasn't much, it did give him the look of quite possibly, maybe being twenty-one years old.

"Fine, but we're going out of town this time. Too close of a call last time at the Q Mart." Andrew said. He was referring to the last time he went in to the one gas station in the Village and bought beer. That night, Andrew handed his fake ID to the clerk, who looked it over like she didn't really care if the name on it was Donald Duck or Mickey Mouse. Andrew proceeded to walk out to the car and put the beer in the trunk of Tanner's car when, just as he was about to get in, Coach Grindell walked up to the car.

"Hey boys, what are you guys up to this fine evening?" asked the head baseball coach.

All the boys tried to act like there weren't two cases of Busch Light in the trunk and that they had pure intentions this evening when Chris said, "Not much, coach, how about you?"

"Just filling up the tank for a fishing trip up north tomorrow. You boys look a little shocked to see me. Everything all right?" he asked.

"Great, coach, just surprised us is all," replied Andrew.

"Okay then…well, have a good night and don't do anything stupid. We need all you boys eligible for baseball season this summer," Grindell said with a wink as he walked away from the car and in to the gas station.

The boys took a collective sigh of relief and then took off out of the parking lot, laughing at how close they were to getting busted.

Chapter Two

1944

"No way, Earl! There's no way I'm doing it. Do you know how much trouble you can get in for that? Never mind the fact that you might get yourself—or both of us, for that matter—killed!" said Victor as he struggled to keep from yelling.

"Vic, buddy, listen to yourself. You're getting way too worked up about this. There are so many of these things around here that no one is going to notice one missing. Besides, all that extra cash would sure be nice, now, wouldn't it?"

"Well, maybe you're right. I just think it's too risky is all," replied Victor.

"Vic, have I ever steered you wrong?" asked Earl.

"Actually, several times!" said Victor as they both laughed.

Both men worked for the Ashbelle Company for the last ten years and were close by any measure: best man in each other's wedding, played on the company bowling team together, hung out with each other on the weekends, best friends.

The Ashbelle Company produced electrical components and had been top-notch at producing them for nearly seventy-five years. When World War II broke out, though, the Ashbelle Company, for reasons both patriotic and fiscally rewarding, had begun producing bombs for the war effort.

Earlier in the year, Earl had gone to Milwaukee to visit his brother, Lenny. Lenny was Earl's older brother by two years and was someone who Earl had always looked up to. They shared many features, both physical and ability-wise, but Lenny was not the "shift-working factory-type" as he liked to tell Earl; this had led to Lenny having some rough patches in his life, including some prison time after participating in different scams with some of his "business associates," as he liked to call them. He had occasionally tried to pull Earl in either by asking directly for help or by asking for money.

Earl had always declined. He loved Lenny and would do anything to help him, but he knew that he had it pretty good—a pretty wife, two beautiful kids, and a great job—and he didn't want to put any of it in jeopardy.

That, however, did not stop Lenny from constantly running "opportunities" by Earl.

As they sat on Lenny's ramshackle porch that summer evening drinking whiskey, Lenny said, "How's everything going, brother?"

The way he asked made Earl feel suspicious, like he was about to be offered up another "opportunity".

"Can't complain. Why do you ask?" asked Earl suspiciously.

"Can't complain, huh? Perfectly happy with everything?" pushed Lenny.

"Yeah, Lenny, I mean I'm good all around. Life is good," replied Earl.

"Even after missing out on that beautiful piece of land you had your eye on up north?" pushed Lenny.

Lenny was referring to a beautiful two hundred-acre piece of hunting land that Earl had been hunting on, with the former owner's permission, for years about fifty miles from the Wisconsin-Michigan border. Last year, the owner, an aging widower, had finally decided to sell the land. He told Earl that he was ready to move south to live with his daughter in Florida where the winter couldn't touch him. Although sad to hear it, Earl was excited because he saw his opportunity to own what he had coveted for so long.

After hunting one day, Earl had come back to the small house on the land and asked the owner straight out if he could buy the land; the owner looked down, sighed, and said that he'd love to sell the land to him, but that there were several offers already on the table. Earl asked, with a lump in his throat, what these offers were and, as he feared, they were higher than he could afford. He couldn't match the offers that had come in which were mainly from wealthy Chicago businessmen who, he assumed, just wanted the land for a cabin and had no idea how great it truly was.

After he sadly told the owner that he couldn't even make him an offer close to those Chicago ones, Earl left feeling a mixture of anger and sadness knowing that he'd never see that land again.

"Lenny, I'm not going to lie, losing that land to a bunch of rich Chicago assholes really chapped my ass. If I had had some more dough, that land would've been mine and eventually my kids and their kids and on and on. Don't get me wrong, my job pays well and it's a great company to work for, but what I wouldn't give sometimes to be one of those Chicago guys with extra cash just lying around," finished Earl as he slammed his remaining whiskey and poured himself another glass.

"Well, little brother, as it so happens, I have a way to make that happen for you," said Lenny.

"Make what happen? How?" replied Earl.

"Make it so you have extra cash lying around so next time a prime piece of land comes on the market, you've got the scratch to pick it up even if you're competing with some Chicago assholes," said Lenny with a smile on his face.

Earl stared at Lenny and wanted to say "not interested in whatever it is, Lenny," but after recounting the whole story with the land, he realized how upset he still was and how he might as well hear Lenny out.

"Okay Lenny, whatcha got?" asked Earl.

"Well, last year, when I was in the pen for that fraud charge, I met a guy who works in the...let's say import/export business," began Lenny.

"Import/export business? Like drugs?" asked Earl.

"No, I'm done with that stuff. This associate of mine happens to be in the business of transporting certain, shall we say, war products from one country to another," whispered Lenny.

"Okay, go on," said Earl.

"So one day, this associate of mine is telling me how once he gets out, which was about two months before me, he's all set up with his uncle on a big job. So I asked him what kind of job and he says that his uncle is looking to move explosives out of the U.S. to non-Axis countries, meaning that none of the stuff would go to America's enemies, but instead to countries in Africa or somewhere who will pay good money to, I don't know, have good stuff to defend themselves should the war expand or something. Anyhow, he asked if I would be interested and I said that not only would I be, but that I know a guy who might be able to help...and that guy, my friend, is you," said Lenny while pointing his finger at Earl.

"Why me?" asked Earl as he finished another shot of whiskey.

"Because, baby brother, the Ashbelle Company, as you're well aware, is a pretty major producer of bombs in the country right now with nice government contracts to kick out basically as many bombs as they can to help beat the crap out of Adolf. It occurred to me that with that many bombs lying around, sneaking one out may not be all that difficult," Lenny said with an intense look on his face. "What do you say?"

Earl ran his hands through his hair and said, "Lenny, I don't know, man. I mean, you're right in that they are all over the place and it could probably be done, but you're looking at a whole shitload of risk. I mean, Lenny, that's treason!"

"I understand, brother, and I don't want to involve you in anything you don't want to do. But I'm just saying, do this one time, and you'll be able to afford any hunting land you want," Lenny said in his typical salesman-like fashion.

Since that night, Earl had been constantly thinking about what Lenny had said. He'd sit in his rocking chair at night after his wife and kids had gone to bed and keep going back and forth between doing it and not. *On the one hand,* he thought, *don't be silly, you have it pretty good. Are you willing to risk it all? On the other hand,* he thought, *I could easily get away with it and having that extra cash would bring that hunting land, and probably anything else I want, within my grasp.*

Then, one night at dinner, he got a call from Lenny, who said that his associate was getting antsy and that he wanted an answer from Earl soon. Earl knew he couldn't keep putting it off and decided he needed to "man up" and make a decision. He waited until the house was quiet and he called Lenny and let him know he was in.

Chapter Three

1997

"Hey Trev, pass me a beer," said Andrew as the four guys sat comfortably on top of the high school that Friday night with a case of Busch Light and some cigars.

For years, high schoolers in Ashbelle had been climbing up on top of the school to party. It was relatively easy to do; the building was only two stories tall and had several areas that were flat and easy to climb on to. Not only that, but with the school being pretty much on the edge of town, no one could really see kids climbing up there, so no one alerted the cops to anything. There were a few houses that could see the back of the school, but they either didn't notice or didn't care.

"It was a real bitch getting these lawn chairs up here, but totally worth it," laughed Tanner.

"I love it up here. I'll bet you kids have been sneaking up here since forever to drink some beer and who knows what else," said Chris.

"Yeah, just got to keep a look out for the cop," said Trev.

It was a well-known fact that the Ashbelle PD had one officer on patrol at any given time. This allowed for partying teenagers to get away with quite a bit, as they knew that once they saw the police drive by, that they wouldn't see any police for quite a while.

"Hey, once we empty this case, let's go play some drunk tennis," said Chris.

"Hell yeah!" replied the three guys simultaneously.

An hour or so later when the beer was gone and the cigars were smoked, the four guys started to make their way down from on top of the school.

"Good thing there's all these ladders. I need something to hold on to right now," said Tanner with somewhat slurred speech.

As the guys made it to ground level, they started to walk toward the tennis courts that were located behind the school at the bottom of a decent-sized hill.

"All right, last one to the tennis courts gets the rapid fire treatment!" yelled Chris as the boys took off in a sprint.

Approaching the tennis courts in the lead, Trev lost his footing on the wet grass, fell, and rolled down the hill on to the edge of the court. "Forgot how slippery it'd be," he said to himself.

The other three intentionally slid down the hill and hit the court about the exact same time, with Andrew just a second behind.

"Damn it!" yelled Andrew as they all laughed.

"You all right, bud?" asked Chris, looking at a crumpled Trev on the court.

"Yeah man, I'm good," said Trev as he sat up with a big smile on his face. "I won."

The boys proceeded over to the storage unit that held the tennis equipment. It was locked, but Chris and Tanner were stars on the school tennis team and knew where their coach hid the key. They pulled out four rackets and as many balls as they could find. Drunk tennis was somewhat like regular tennis, except that the point was to hit your opponents with as many balls as possible as hard as possible and you couldn't go behind the service line, so it was all pretty up close and painful.

Before they began, though, it was time for Andrew's punishment: the rapid-fire treatment. As Andrew lined up against the fence, each guy got a chance to hit four balls at him from about twenty feet away. Like usual, he caught a couple to the head and neck, but nothing that would hurt that bad...as long as you covered your privates.

After the boys had played drunk tennis, they went over to the hillside to have one more cigar before heading back to Chris's house.

"I can't believe we're all going to be out of here in a few months," said Andrew.

"I know, man, it's sad but exciting, you know?" replied Tanner.

The four guys had been going to school together basically since kindergarten, and even though they rarely said it, none of them could imagine life without each other. Sure, they sometimes fought and sometimes hung out with other groups, but they were always tight-knit.

Ashbelle was the type of town where everyone knew everyone—their parents, their siblings, and even their pet—so it wasn't rare to see freshman and sophomores at seniors' parties. It was kind of an initiation-type thing: Seniors would give you a little shit then hand you a beer.

Andrew remembered his first high school party; he had been hanging out with Trevor, Tanner, and Chris just watching TV or something when Chris said that there was a party going on at some girl's house. The guys, being freshman, were a little nervous about going, but decided to check it out. When they arrived, the older kids did what the older kids do and gave them some shit like "Isn't it past your bedtime?" and "Does your mommy know you're here?" but it was all in good fun. This town looked out for each other, even the high school kids.

After being at the party for an hour or so, Andrew was sitting on the couch with Tanner when two cool seniors walked in with a backpack full of beer. The senior class that year was a cool class full of athletic, fun-loving guys and hot girls. One of the senior guys who had just showed up was named Tim Larkin, but he was referred to as Lark. He was an all-around athlete, but not one of the most athletic guys in his class. He was the kind of guy that everyone wanted at their party: fun, a little loud, and always ready to get after it. Andrew's older brother was a junior at the time, but he hung out with Lark and most the other senior guys, as the guys in his class weren't really athletic and he was.

To Andrew and Tanner's surprise, Lark walked up to the couch they were on and handed each of them a can of Keystone Light and said, "Drink up, boys."

Andrew and Tanner maybe didn't want the beers, but to turn them down would've been social suicide, so they opened them up and slammed them the best they could.

"Nice job, ladies" said Lark as he walked away. The boys looked at each other and Tanner said, "That tasted like shit."

"Yeah," replied Andrew, "but that was pretty cool."

"Listen to you guys, you sound like a bunch of little bitches," said Chris, bringing Andrew out of his daydream. Chris then looked at Trev and said, "You and me, brother, race to the top of the hill?"

"You're on," said Trev as they both began the perilous run up the hill. Not surprisingly, both slipped and struggled to make it up to the top, with Trev getting there first thanks to being six foot five inches tall with a ridiculously long stride, and because Chris had slipped about halfway up. Trev looked down about to give Chris shit about not finishing when he saw that, oddly enough, Chris appeared to be stuck to the hill.

"You all right, bud?" asked Trev as he looked halfway down the hill at Chris.

"First of all, ow. Second of all, I'm fine. This is weird, though, dude, but my arm is like seriously stuck," replied Chris.

"You're stuck? Like in to the hill? Are you that drunk?" asked Andrew as he and Tanner looked up at Chris and Trev from below.

"No dude, just come help me," said Chris.

Andrew, Trev, and Tanner got to Chris, expecting that he was messing around, but realized his arm was buried in to the hill up past his elbow. After a few seconds of tugging, they were able to pull Chris's arm out of hillside.

"What the hell?" said Andrew. "That's not normal."

"How the hell is that even possible?" asked Tanner.

"Maybe it's like a sinkhole or something?" said Trev.

"Yeah, but those are usually on the ground, not in a hillside," said Tanner.

"Must be hollow back there, though, for some reason. Maybe someone buried something in the hill or something," said Andrew.

"Let's see," said Chris as he and Trev started tearing away chunks of grass and dirt around where Chris's arm had gone in.

Fortunately, the guys had a flashlight; they always brought one when climbing on top of the school. "Turn that thing on and point it here, Tanner, will you?" said Chris.

Chris took the flashlight from Tanner and pointed it in to the hole they had dug in to the hillside. "Can't really see anything, but it's definitely hollow back there. Andrew, hand me a rock. I want to try something."

Andrew looked around, grabbed a decent-sized rock by the tennis court, and handed it to Chris. Chris threw the rock in to the hole and heard it hit something with a small clangy sound. "One more," said Chris.

This time, Chris threw the rock harder in to the hole and the guys all heard a definite clang —the kind of sound that only came from something metal.

"The hell was that?" asked Trev.

"We've got to get a shovel and see what the hell is back there," said Chris.

The boys hopped in Andrew's car and drove to Trev's house.

"Shovels are in the garage, but be quiet. My dad's probably sleeping on the couch."

The boys could see the TV on through the window and knew that Trev was probably right.

The boys went around to the side door of the detached garage to avoid the loud sound the garage door made when it opened or closed.

"Door's locked, dude," said Tanner to Trev.

"Key's under the mat, and quiet the hell down," replied Trev.

"Solid hiding spot," quipped Chris sarcastically. Trev ignored him.

After entering the garage, Trev said to not turn on the light, so they used the flashlight to find some shovels on the far wall. Even though they had the flashlight, of course Andrew kicked an oilcan and Chris fell over the garbage bin, making a loud noise.

"What the hell?" hissed Trev.

"Sorry," they both said.

"Let's just get the shovels and get the hell out of here."

The boys grabbed a couple of shovels and managed to get out of the garage without banging in to or tripping over anything else. Just as they locked the door back up, they saw Trev's dad standing on the porch in his robe. He looked at them, they looked at him, and finally he said, "I don't even want to know why you have shovels at this time of night, but if any of you go to jail, I'm not bailing any of your asses out—especially yours, Trev." He walked back inside.

They boys put the shovels in the car and headed straight back to the hole they had dug with their hands.

On the walk there, Tanner said, "What do you guys think it is back there?"

"Don't know," said Trev.

"Probably just some old piece of crap toy or something," said Andrew.

"Maybe it's gold!" said Chris.

The boys reached the hillside and started digging with the shovels. Chris and Andrew dug while Trev and Tanner were on watch to see if anyone was coming, like a dog walker or the cop. After about ten minutes, they had made a big enough hole where they were able to see what had caused the clang sound from the rock.

"Is that a…no, can't be," said Andrew with a strange look on his face.

"A what?" asked Trev.

"Well, it's still got shit all over it, but it looks like a door," replied Andrew.

"Sure looks like one to me," said Chris, "but what the hell is a door doing in the hillside?"

"Wait!" said Andrew excitedly.

"What?" Trev asked.

"Do you guys remember what Winters was saying in class today about the tunnels from WWII?"

"I was sleeping," said Tanner.

"I was thinking about that hot girl in front of me," said Trev.

"Yeah," replied Chris, "but he said there weren't any of those around here."

"That anyone knows of," replied Andrew.

"Do you really think?" asked Tanner after Andrew had explained to him and Trev what Chris and him were talking about.

"I don't know, but let's find out," said Chris. "Turn off that flashlight. We don't need the cop driving by here and seeing us."

After an hour or so, the boys had got the door completely uncovered. They realized they had no idea how to get the door open.

"It's an exit door, so there's no handle on it," said Andrew.

"Then how the hell are we going to get it open?" asked Tanner.

Hitting it with shovels several times had no affect on the door, which was clearly made from some solid material.

"Should we shoot it?" asked Tanner.

"No way, man. It'd just ricochet back at us," said Chris.

"And be way too freaking loud," said Trev.

"I've got it," said Andrew. "You know how my dad was in the army, right? Well, he was a demolition specialist and one thing he keeps from then is a handheld blowtorch. He's told me like a dozen times never to touch it as it gets hot enough to burn you 'like you don't even want to know,' but that it also gets hot enough to melt almost any metal."

"I like it," said Chris. "Let's go."

"Trev and I will stay here," said Tanner.

"Cool, be back in a bit," said Andrew as he and Chris left to go get the blowtorch.

Fortunately, Andrew's parents were out of town for some work convention, so he was easily able to take the blowtorch. "My dad would seriously kill me if he knew we were even touching this," said Andrew as he looked at the blowtorch.

"Fine, I'll touch it," said a smiling Chris as he grabbed it and took it to the car.

About twenty minutes later, Chris and Andrew were back with the blowtorch. "Go ahead," said Trev.

"I don't know how to use it," replied Andrew.

"Give me that thing," said Tanner as he grabbed it, flicked the switch to start, and watched in awe with the other guys as it lit up a fluorescent orange in a matter of seconds.

"What the hell am I doing?" he said as he slowly touched it to the door.

After a minute or so, smoke started to come off of the door, and the blowtorch moved in slightly. Tanner kept it going until it had actually, shockingly, gone through the door.

"Hell yes!" shouted Chris.

"Keep it down! And turn that shit off, or we're going to get spotted!" snapped Andrew at him.

"All right, sorry. Good thing there's like no houses around here," replied Chris.

"A few, but they're all dark," said Tanner.

It took another hour or so of all the guys taking turns until they had made a big enough hole to reach one of their heads through the hole.

With the flashlight in his mouth, Chris stuck his head through the hole, making sure the metal was cool first. After a minute or so, he pulled his head out and said, "There's a wheel on the inside of the door like on those old-time safes that I bet will turn and open this thing up, but I can't reach it."

"Trev, you try it. Your go-go Gadget arm should be able to reach it," said Andrew, referring to the Inspector Gadget cartoon that they had all watched growing up.

"Being six foot five has its advantages," said Trev as he grasped the wheel.

"Can you turn it?" said Andrew.

"Hold on, hold on..." said Trev with his teeth clenched. "Got it."

Trev had managed to turn the wheel and the door popped open just a hair. Andrew grabbed the side of the door and pulled on it hard until it had opened enough to allow them to sneak through.

"Sweet," said Tanner.

"All right, boys, let's check it out," said Chris.

"Whoa, let's just hold on a second," said Andrew.

"Man up!" replied Tanner.

"All right, assholes, let's check it out," said Andrew.

After the boys had all snuck through the door, making sure to bring the blowtorch and shovels in with them, Andrew shut it, hoping that no one would see the pile of dirt outside it and come and investigate.

Once inside, the boys immediately noticed the smell. "Gross, smells like shit," said Chris.

"Probably hasn't been opened in decades. No wonder it smells," replied Tanner.

The boys turned on their one flashlight again and started to shine it all around them. They could tell they were in a tunnel, but couldn't see very far down it.

"What do you think is in there? Think it goes to the factory?" asked Trev.

"Maybe," said Andrew. "That'd make sense based on what Winters said in class today."

"Let's go," said Tanner and the boys began to head further in to the tunnel.

It was slow going, but the boys kept moving down the tunnel in a single-file line with Chris in the lead.

"Even with this flashlight, I can't see shit," said Chris.

"Just take small steps," replied Andrew.

The boys had gone another fifty feet or so when all of a sudden Chris tripped and fell, which caused Andrew and Tanner to trip on him and to fall themselves.

"The hell, Chris?" yelled Tanner.

"Get off me!" yelled Chris to Andrew.

The whole mess caused the flashlight to go flying, but fortunately it stayed on and Trev walked slowly to retrieve it, trying to avoid tripping on whatever it was that had caused the three other guys to fall. Upon reaching the flashlight, Trev turned it back on the three guys, who were all standing now, brushing themselves off.

"Trev, what's up, man? You look like you've seen a ghost?" asked Andrew.

"I think I pretty much have. Look at what you all tripped over," said Trev as he lowered the beam of light down on to the skeleton on the ground.

The three other guys gave a collective "holy shit!" as they all instinctively took a few steps back.

"Dude, we have to get out of here," said Tanner.

"T, it's not going to get up and chase you. Just relax," said Chris.

"Let's check it out," said Trev.

The guys approached the body and knelt down next to it. "This thing's clearly been here for a long, long time," said Andrew.

The body was a skeleton at this point. The skin had long since went away. It was dressed in clothes that had faded with time, but still remained intact. It didn't look like any animals or anything had made their way in and chewed on it or anything. The tunnel was basically a sealed tomb.

As the boys scanned the body with the flashlight, moving from toes to head, they saw that it was clearly a police officer by the belt, the badge, the stripes.

"Wilskie," said Chris as he knelt by the skeleton. "Ashbelle P.D."

"You guys ever hear of an Ashbelle cop getting killed or gone missing or anything?" said Andrew.

"Actually yeah," said Trev. "My dad said something about it one time, but when I asked him what he was talking about, he said don't worry about it. It was a long time ago. Dudes, check it out," said Trev as he moved the flashlight up to the skull.

"Holy shit, this dude was murdered. Look!" yelled Chris as he pointed at the skeleton's forehead.

"Looks like a hole from a bullet," said Andrew as they looked at the skull and saw that a chunk was missing from the forehead area.

"Maybe it was a suicide," said Tanner.

"If it was, the gun would be near the body, but I don't see a gun anywhere, so I don't think so," said Andrew.

"Crazy. Makes you wonder what the hell happened" said Trev. "Like what was he doing down here? Did he catch someone in here and they shot him? Or did he know something he shouldn't have?

"What do we do now?" asked Tanner. "Do we go to the cops?"

All four of the guys just looked down, unsure of what to do next.

"Well, I think we have to, but let's cover this door back up first. We don't need some little kid or something coming in here," said Andrew.

Chapter Four

1944

"So what's the plan, Earl?" whispered Victor as he and Earl sat down in the lunchroom at the Ashbelle Company.

Earl looked around to make sure no one else was listening and said, "Have you heard the rumors that there are tunnels running away from the factory?"

"Sure, but I've heard they're just that: rumors," replied Victor.

"Well apparently, they're not just rumors; it's true. My brother has it on good authority that back in '41 during that time when they mysteriously shut the factory down for two weeks— remember that?"

"Of course. An unexpected two-week vacation for everybody while still getting paid? That was great!" said Victor as he took a bite of his bologna sandwich.

"Well apparently, that two weeks was when they put in the tunnels," said Earl.

"Earl, tunnels like that would take more than two weeks to build," replied Victor.

"For sure, but two weeks would be enough time to dig the start of them and cover up the entryways with no one the wiser when we all got back.

And, with as loud as it is around here, they could easily have finished them with no one knowing about it."

"I guess so," admitted Victor.

"Anyway, my brother's associate somehow got his hands on a map of the tunnel system—where they begin, where they go, including where they pop out in the Village. With that information, we can plan a way to get one of those bombs out of here. You and I are going to meet my brother just outside of town tomorrow after work to take a look at that map."

"Okay, Earl, sounds good…I guess. One last thing, Earl, if I go through with this, I don't want 40 percent, I want fifty-fifty," said Victor in a surprisingly tough manner not common with his personality. "If we get caught, it's my ass on the line, too."

Earl leaned back in his chair and thought about it. Victor was referring to Earl's cut of the profits; Earl had thought it was fair that he should get 10 percent more than Victor, as it was him who was giving Victor the opportunity—kind of a finder's fee—but he needed Vic, and so a few seconds later, a big smile appeared on his face. He leaned across the table, slapped Victor on the shoulder, and said, "Fair enough, buddy. Hunting land for both of us."

Chapter Five

It was mid-morning on Saturday and Chief David Preston was sitting behind his desk at the Ashbelle Police Department looking over some recent traffic stop numbers. Preston was a big man, but not fat by any means. He continued to work out daily even at forty-seven years old as he always had; he liked to keep fit for several reasons, but mainly because he didn't want to become the stereotypical out-of-shape cop that people liked to make fun of. He also encouraged his officers to stay fit, not only so they could also avoid the ridicule, but he believed that an officer who looked built was much more likely to make someone think twice about committing a crime than a cop that looked like Barney Fife or the Michelin Man.

Preston had grown up in Ashbelle and loved the Village. He had started out of college as a patrol officer in the Village and had worked his way up to chief, just as his father had. He was an all-state athlete at Ashbelle High and always knew he wanted to follow in his dad's footsteps. He had college classmates and friends from the police academy that would frequently rib him for working in such a sleepy town; they'd say things like "Don't you feel like you're wasting your talent?" or "Why don't you come work for a real police department and fight real crime?" Sometimes those comments hurt, but he never considered going anywhere else; he liked being responsible for keeping Ashbelle a safe place where kids could play outside and you could walk around town at any time of day and feel safe.

The police station itself wasn't huge, but it was well kept and cozy, a reflection of how the Village residents felt about their police department. Many similarly sized towns didn't have their own police force, opting to rely on the sheriff's office for patrol to save money, but there was a pride in the Village of seeing cars with Ashbelle on the side of them and knowing the chief and officers personally and vice versa.

Preston sat back in his chair and started to daydream, as he often did, about memories of growing up in the Village. He was in the middle of re-living winning the football conference championship his senior year when he was shaken out of it by the buzzer on his desk.

"Chief Preston?" buzzed a voice from the police station's front desk.

"Yes Sharon," said Preston as he gathered himself.

"There's some boys here to see you, but they won't tell me what about," replied Sharon in an annoyed tone.

"Okay Sharon, thanks. Send them in," said Preston.

It actually wasn't that rare that Village residents stopped in to speak with him; most the time it was people his own age or older who either wanted to chat about their shared past or to let him know of something they thought he should be aware of going on in the Village, such as kids partying here, people speeding there, suspicious vehicles, and so forth. It was odd, however, to have high schoolers stop in, so he was immediately interested in finding out what the boys wanted to see him about.

Chief Preston got up from his comfortable chair as the four boys walked in to his office.

"Have a seat, boys. What can I do for you today?" said Preston as he pointed to the couch and chairs in his office opposite his desk.

The boys all looked at each other and then Andrew said, "Mind if we shut the door?"

The reasons Andrew wanted to shut the door was that it was common knowledge in the Village that Sharon at the front desk was quite a gossip and frequently eavesdropped on conversations going on in Preston's office. Preston was also aware of this, but even so, he usually kept his door open to keep it a less-formal atmosphere, unlike most police departments that seemed stiff and unwelcoming.

"Sure, no problem," replied Preston as he got up and shut the door, much to Sharon's chagrin.

Preston took a seat behind his desk and again asked the boys what they wanted to talk to him about. Chris and Andrew had taken the two seats in front of the desk, while Trev and Tanner took seats on the couch.

After a minute of silence from the boys, Preston asked, "Is everything okay, guys?"

"Yeah, well, no," said Chris, looking nervously down at the ground.

Andrew spoke first. "We, ah, well, we found something last night and it was pretty wild and also pretty freaky."

"Pretty wild and pretty freaky. Okay, you've got my attention," said Preston.

"We were partying, I mean hanging out, last night on top of, I mean near the school," said Chris.

Preston laughed quietly to himself as he knew what the kids were doing and where. He, too, had partied on top of the school when he was their age; it was a tradition that went way back. He tended to take the same approach to it that his father had: Short of destruction or violence, he and his officers looked the other way. They figured they'd rather have the high school kids stay in town where it was safe and they could keep an eye on them from a distance. Ashbelle, like most small towns, had its partying spots everyone knew about that had been used for years.

"And we ended up by the tennis courts and, and I know this'll sound weird, but we ended up finding a door in the hill," said Andrew, looking down as if he knew how stupid and unbelievable what he had just said sounded.

"I'm sorry, did you say a door in the hillside?" asked Preston.

"Yeah, but that's not what we're here about," replied Andrew.

"Yeah, we're here about the dead police officer we found in the tunnel behind the door!" shouted Chris a little too loudly.

"What?" replied Preston. "Okay, okay, let's start from the beginning.

So the boys told Preston everything that had happened from how they found the door, to how they opened it, to finding the skeleton in the tunnel.

After hearing this seemingly elaborate tale, Preston leaned back in his chair and said, "You know when I was a kid, my dad told me the story of a Village police officer who just went missing one day. He told me how he remembered going out with his parents and others all around the village looking for the officer. People said he just never finished his shift and he was never heard from again. Some people didn't know if he just took off, which seemed unlikely as he had a family, but you never know, it happens. Anyway, people scoured everywhere and nothing, and I mean nothing, was ever found—no car, no body, no witnesses, nothing. As far as I know, he was the only officer this department ever lost in the line of duty. Of course, no one's sure if he was lost in the actual line of duty. I also had heard rumors that there were tunnels underneath the Village, but my uncle, who worked at the Ashbelle Company, said that that was nonsense. I'm going to need you guys to show me the tunnel, the body, everything. We're going to have to wait until it's dark, though, or we'll bring on too much attention. I want you boys to go about your day like it's a normal Saturday and then meet me behind the school around 10:00, understood?

The boys all nodded.

"And two very important things to not do today. First, don't tell anyone, and I mean anyone, about what you found last night—not your parents, not your friends, not your girlfriends—and two, do not under any circumstances go by the tunnel until we meet, got it?

The boys all nodded, got up, and left. As Preston watched the boys walk toward their vehicle, he leaned back in his chair and thought to himself that either these boys were playing a very well-thought-out prank on him or they just fell ass backward in to solving two of the biggest mysteries that had ever enveloped the tiny Village of Ashbelle.

Although he had told the boys to act like this was any other normal Saturday, he had to keep reminding himself of that.

As he walked out of his office for one of his daily drives around the Village, Sharon rolled her chair directly in front of him, blocking his way out, and said, "So Chief, what was that all about?"

"Oh nothing, Sharon, just local boys telling me about some things I should know about," replied Preston, trying to look like he hadn't just heard the most shocking news of his life.

"In other words, you're not going to tell me. Okay, that's fine, but good old Sharon always figures out what's going. Remember that," Sharon said as she slowly rolled her chair out of Preston's way and back behind her desk.

Preston walked past Sharon chuckling and headed out toward his cruiser.

Preston did these drive throughs, as he liked to call them, several times per shift to not only keep an eye on things but to also get a pulse of what was going on and to remind Village residents that he wasn't a chief that just sat in his office all day. He wanted people to come up and talk to him as he rolled by. Neither he nor his officers could know everything, so he relied heavily on people in the Village to tell him things. He also wanted the kids to come up and talk to him as well. Kids who were taught at an early age that the police weren't the enemy were more likely to stay out of trouble and share what they knew. He didn't know that for a fact, of course, but he felt it in his bones.

Preston went a little slower than normal this time as he drove by the tennis courts. As usual this time of year, there were kids playing tennis and running or rolling up and down the hill. He parked his car on the curb, got out, and leaned on the passenger's side of the hood to give the appearance of saying hi to the kids, which he did, but the real reason he was there was to determine if he could see this "door in the hill." Part of him wanted to see it so he knew that the boys he met with before weren't lying, but part of him dreaded seeing it as it would definitely draw attention from children and parents alike. Fortunately, as Preston scanned the hill, he didn't see anything. The hill was dotted with trees, which could have been blocking his view, but if what the boys told him was true, he was very impressed at their foresight to cover the door back up and also what an amazing job they had done. Satisfied, but still not sure what was true and what was not, Preston waved good-bye and slid back in to his cruiser. He looked at his watch. It was only 1:00 P.M. This was going to be a long day, he thought to himself.

◄○►

It was 10:00, and Preston was waiting behind the school for the boys to arrive. He was a little nervous, as he wasn't in uniform or his police cruiser since he had left work and had gone home to change, and he wondered what excuse he might give a random dog walker who asked what he was doing there. He decided that, if that were to happen, he would say something vague, like that he had just got a tip about something that he couldn't really talk about. It was weak, but it would work, he thought. He looked at his watch again: 10:05. *Darn kids*, he thought to himself. *If they've set me up, I'm going to be pissed*. Just as he went to look at his watch again, he saw Andrew's black Blazer rolling up the parking lot.

He hoped that no one had stumbled by the tunnel door yet. The boys appeared to have done a good job covering it up, at least from a distance. But having not seen it close up yet, he hoped that no kids or anyone had discovered it.

Preston watched as Andrew did a big circle around the parking lot and then pulled up next to Preston's driver's side.

"Sorry Chief. Wasn't sure that was you. Didn't recognize your car," said Andrew.

"No worries. I was beginning to think this was all a hoax to make me look like an idiot," replied Preston. "Let's both park a ways apart at the end of the parking lot away from the tennis courts. Don't want to draw any suspicion. Also, you guys haven't told anyone about this yet, have you?"

Andrew shook his head no, as did Trevor, Tanner, and Chris.

"Great," said Preston. "Thank you for handling this like men."

After they had both parked, Preston and the boys met up at the top of the hill. Preston handed each boy a flashlight and told them to not use them unless they absolutely had to—at least until they were inside the tunnel with the door closed behind them. Although out of uniform and off-duty, Preston was armed. He couldn't be sure that no one else had discovered the tunnel yet and he wanted to be able to handle any situation that may arise.

Preston said, "All right, boys, show me what you've got to show me." He was nervous, but also excited. This was a crazy situation and he wasn't exactly sure how he'd handle it, but he wanted to be strong for the boys. After all, they had come to him with this info instead of blabbing it all over town, and he appreciated that.

The group began to slowly make their way down the hill. It hadn't rained today, so thankfully it wasn't that slippery. As they got about halfway down, the boys stopped and Chris pointed to the hillside and said, "Here it is."

Preston was disappointed when he saw the area up close. He wasn't sure how he hadn't seen it before during the day, but there was dirt loose around the door—not a great covering job. He was now really concerned someone else had seen it.

The boys could tell that Preston was a little upset and Tanner asked him, "Why are you shaking your head, Chief?"

"Sorry, guys. I was just hoping this doorway was covered up really well like you guys said you had done. Look at all this loose dirt, and you can even see part of the door."

The boys looked bewildered as they looked at the door and then each other. Preston was right: It looked like a crappy job and not at all like how they had left it.

Seeing the perplexed look on the boys' faces, Preston asked, "What is it, guys?"

Finally Chris said, "Chief, we did a really thorough job of covering this up when we left."

"Yeah, it didn't look this shitty when we were done with it," said Trev.

"Yeah, you have to believe us!" said an irritated Tanner.

"Hmmm, I'm as confused as you guys because when I was across the tennis courts this afternoon, I couldn't see anything at all on the hillside. It couldn't have looked like this. Even from that distance, I would've seen this. Also, there were several people around here at that time. Someone would've seen it for sure."

"So you do believe us?" said Andrew.

"I do, but that means that someone's been here recently, which is not good. Well, we'll have to deal with that later. We're here now, so let's get in this thing before any one sees us."

Everyone took one last look around and started clearing away the dirt and grass left covering the door. Like before, Trev reached in the hole they had created and turned the wheel. The door popped open an inch, and they opened it just enough so they could all sneak in.

The boys began to enter the tunnel, but Preston just stood there for a second staring bewildered at the door in the hill. As he looked at the metal door, he felt himself shook as he was looking at proof that the legends he had heard growing up of tunnels hidden throughout the Village that were built in case the factory was going to be destroyed by German or Japanese bombers were actually true. He never believed those stories and he couldn't believe that no one, until now, had actually discovered where one of these tunnels was.

"Chief!" whispered Chris. "You all right?"

"Ah, yeah, just this is crazy is all," replied Preston.

"Crazy and scary," said Tanner.

After regaining his composure, Preston said, "All right, let's get this door open and take a look at this body."

Preston snuck in behind the boys, making sure to close the door tightly behind them.

"Okay, boys, we don't have much time. That door is pretty visible from the outside now, so let's take a look and get out of here. Flashlights on."

The group began down the tunnel. The boys let Preston take the lead this time. After about five minutes of walking down the tunnel, Preston said to the boys, "Okay, where's the body?"

All four boys looked at each other dumbfounded.

"C'mon guys, what's going on here?" Preston said in a somewhat accusatory voice as if this body story were maybe just something the boys either made up to get him down here or they thought they saw something that wasn't actually there.

"It was here, Chief. I swear, we all saw it. Tripped over it, actually," stammered Chris.

"Boys, and I'm not trying to get you in trouble, but had you guys maybe had too much to drink last night and may have thought that whatever you possibly saw was a body?" asked Preston. "I don't want to suggest you all are up to something, but there's no body here."

"What the hell?" said Trev. All the boys were thinking the same thing.

Preston stood up straight and looked each boy in the eye. He wanted to believe the boys, but knew that occasionally teenage boys could get all excited and get their facts wrong, even in a situation like this. "Now boys, this tunnel is awesome. Very cool you discovered it. But I need to know if there was a body or not. Having a murder on my hands or not is a huge deal."

"Chief, I—all of us—swear on our lives that there was a body here in what looked like a police uniform," said Tanner. "I don't understand…"

After a few moments of confused silence, Preston said. "All right boys, I'll tell you what. Let's get out of here, cover this thing up as well as we can, and go back to the station and file an official report," said Preston.

The boys all nodded and followed Preston out of the tunnel. Fortunately, Preston still didn't see anyone out walking a dog or going for a stroll. Once they were all out of the tunnel, they closed the door up tight and spent the next thirty minutes covering the door up the best they could.

"Good job, boys. Someone's going to have to get real close to even notice this ground was disturbed. Let's head back to the cars and I'll meet you at the station in about ten minutes," said Preston.

Once Preston had gone the direction to his car, the boys began to talk among themselves.

"Seriously, what the hell? We all saw that body!" said Chris angrily.

"No doubt," replied Tanner.

"And it wasn't some animal skeleton or anything either," said Trev.

"It was definitely there, and I don't know what the hell happened to it," said Andrew. "I think someone stole it."

"Stole it? For real?" said Tanner.

"How the hell could someone have stolen the body? We just found it last night after how many years of it being here? No one else knows about the tunnel or the body," replied Chris.

"I think he's right," said Trev, "I mean, you all know we didn't leave the door looking that shitty when we left. That means somebody uncovered it and did a piss-poor job covering it back up."

"Probably were in a hurry, too. That's why they did such a shitty job," replied Tanner.

"Okay, but who the hell saw us?" asked Chris.

"And why would they even want the body inside there?" replied Andrew.

"I don't know, but I'm going to find out," said Chris.

The boys all got a little worried after hearing that because Chris was known to do whatever he had to, to get at what he wanted, and he was oftentimes a dumbass in going about doing that. Still worked with the ladies quite often, though.

"Are you now? Okay, well, be careful. This isn't some piece of ass you're going after. This is some serious shit," said Andrew.

"Me? Careful? Always," chuckled Chris.

The boys went back to the police station. Fortunately, Sharon had gone home for the night; she would've loved to tell the whole Village about the four high school seniors coming back late to file reports with the chief.

Once inside Preston's office, the boys were instructed to write down what they had all seen. As Andrew was writing, he thought to himself that Preston was pretty cool; even after what had happened in the tunnel, he never once came out and called them liars or yelled at them, even though he was probably thinking it.

After the boys had finished, Preston said, "All right, boys. Thanks. I'll be in touch. And remember, let's keep this tunnel and everything else a secret for now, just in case there's evidence in there we missed or something. I don't need the whole Village traipsing around in there."

The boys all nodded their heads, walked out of the police station, and hopped in Andrew's Blazer. There was very little conversation as Andrew dropped each of them off.

Chapter Six

1944

Earl and Victor were leaned up against Earl's old pickup truck smoking a cigarette.

"What time's he going to be here?" said Victor impatiently.

"Easy, Vic, he'll be here. What are you so nervous about?" replied Earl.

"Well, maybe I'm nervous because I'm sitting here with you just outside of town after work by this abandoned farmhouse waiting for your crazy brother to bring a classified map showing us how to commit treason!" sniped Victor.

Earl replied, "Vic, listen to me. I get it, but this is easy. Lenny's the one doing most of the illegal stuff and—"

Just then they heard a car squeal in to the farmyard and heard, "Little brother, good to see you again, you son of a bitch!"

"I suppose that's Lenny, right?" said Victor in an annoyed tone to Earl, but Earl didn't have a chance to answer as Lenny slammed the car to a stop right in front of them.

"Nice car, Lenny," said Earl as he looked at the new jet-black Buick Lenny had pulled up in. "How on earth can you afford this thing?"

"Let's just say business is good in the import/export game. You'll be driving one of your own soon enough," replied Lenny.

Lenny got out of the car, threw his sunglasses off, and gave Earl a big bear hug. After releasing his brother from the unnecessarily long and aggressive hug, Lenny pointed at Victor and said, "Who the hell is this guy and what the hell is he doing here?"

"Lenny, calm down. This is Victor. He's my best friend and, more importantly, he works with me at Ashbelle," replied Earl, adding before Lenny could say another word, "He's solid. You don't have to worry about him."

"I don't know, Earl..." said Lenny suspiciously.

"Lenny, I vouch for Victor. He's my best friend and I've been working with him for years now, and besides, we're going to need help getting this thing out of there. Do you know how heavy those bombs are? Besides, Victor knows that factory floor better than anyone," Earl said, trying to ease Lenny's mind. "And his pay will come out of my portion."

Lenny turned and stared at Victor for several seconds before cracking in to a smile and saying, "All right, all right."

Lenny turned around and walked back to the trunk of his car as Victor whispered, "What the heck was that all about? You didn't tell him about me?"

"Not exactly, but it's cool," whispered Earl back.

"Hey, you two, come here. I've got something to show you," said Lenny as he slammed the trunk closed.

Lenny unrolled the map on the trunk and began to show Earl and Victor what their options were. Victor couldn't believe what he was looking at. Not only was it a dangerous and illegal map to have, but it proved what had been suspected by many at the factory and around the Village.

"Here's a map of the entire factory floor, and as you can see, there are four tunnels, one near each corner. The next page shows where each of these tunnels pop out at various points in the Village."

Flipping to the second page out of excitement, a wide-eyed and excited Earl began saying in an amazed voice, "I believed you, but just to see the map of it is crazy. One of them pops out not far from the house we grew up in near Roosevelt Park on the south side. And this one here pops out in the ravine somewhere near the train trestle. This one pops out by the Lutheran Church. And this last one here pops out right behind the school by the tennis courts."

"I know, brother. It is crazy. Couldn't believe it myself at first," said Lenny, flipping back to the first page. "Now, back to the issue at hand. Where on here are the bombs kept?"

"Let me see…" said Earl as he looked at the map.

Victor stepped in, pointed at the map, and said, "They're kept here, in the northwest corner because that's the closest to the shipping bays where they're loaded up and taken away."

"Okay, so let's take a look at the tunnel in that corner, then," said Lenny as he traced his finger over the map to the spot. After flipping back to the second page, he said. "It looks like this one goes under the road, continues under the Patriot Club, and pops out by the tennis courts behind school. Perfect. There are practically no houses over there to worry about someone seeing us."

"I'm surprised they didn't have one just pop out in the Patriot Club. I mean Ashbelle owns the whole thing and all," said Earl.

"Maybe they thought it wasn't far enough away from the factory if it were to get bombed, or maybe it'd be a target itself," said Victor.

The Patriot Club was a boarding house of sorts, built by the Ashbelle Company to house mainly European immigrant men who were recruited and brought over by the company to work in the factory since 1912. The club was a beautiful brick and stone building that was named the Patriot Club due to the fact that, besides being a residence for such men, it was a place that encouraged the foreign workers to learn to love and appreciate America by teaching these men English and by offering classes on American History, American authors, and so forth. The eventual goal was that these men would become proud American citizens. The company even gave men paid time off to take their citizenship tests.

"I'm sure this map is correct and all, but I've spent a lot of time in that corner and I've never seen anything that looks like it would lead to a tunnel, have you, Vic?" said Earl.

"No, I haven't either, but let's take a closer look here. Does the map give any detail on where this mysterious tunnel entrance is exactly?" replied Victor as all three men moved closer to the map.

After a minute, Victor pointed at a small bit of writing on the map near the northwest corner and said, "What does that say right there?"

"It looks like it says JC," replied Earl.

"Like, as in Jesus Christ?" asked a stupefied Lenny.

Rolling his eyes, Victor replied, "I doubt it."

Trying to not let Lenny get upset at Victor, Earl quickly said, "Any idea what 'JC' could mean, Vic?"

"I mean, not that I can think of. All that's over there is some equipment and rows of bombs," said Victor.

In classic form, Lenny took a step back, put his hands up in the air, and yelled, "C'mon guys, use your frickin' brains! We need to figure this shit out in a hurry. We don't have much time!"

"Up yours, Lenny. We're doing the best we can!" yelled Earl back as he shoved Lenny.

That was it. They were back to being ten and twelve years old again. "Oh that's it!" said Lenny as he put Earl in a headlock and wrestled him to the ground.

As the brothers continued to wrestle on the ground, Victor kept looking at the map trying to figure out what "JC" might mean. He went through in his head what was on the factory floor, but then he had a revelation and yelled, "Guys…guys…GUYS!" He had yelled loud enough that both brothers stopped wrestling and stared at the normally meek Victor in astonishment.

"What you got, buddy?" asked Earl while giving Lenny one last elbow to the gut.

"Janitor's closet," said Victor.

"Who gives a crap about a janitor's closet?" said Lenny as he held his ribs where that last elbow from Earl had landed squarely.

Dusting himself off as he got to his feet, Earl said, "Go on, buddy."

Victor replied, "It's really easy to miss, but do you recall that doorway that's about twenty or so feet away from that corner that is painted the exact same color as the wall?"

"Let me think…Yeah, yeah, I know it," replied Earl.

"It says janitor's closet on it, but have you ever in your entire time working there, ever seen anyone go in to it or come out of it?" asked Victor.

"No, but they do cleaning during all the shifts. They could use that one when we're not around," said Earl.

"You could be right, but that has to be it," said Victor.

A now cooled-down Lenny finally said, "Well, why don't you and boy genius check it out at work tomorrow?" as he dusted himself off.

"I will," said Earl. "I'll think of some way to get in that room. What are you going to be up to?"

"I'm going to try and find out exactly where this tunnel pops out," replied Lenny. "I'll meet you guys behind the school after work."

As Lenny was putting the map back in to the trunk, he pointed at Victor and said, "I don't know you, which means I don't trust you. But you seem smart and if my brother vouches for you, we're cool…for now."

Chapter Seven

S am had just sat down in his old, beat-up recliner with a fresh whiskey and Coke in his hand ready to watch some Saturday night baseball when the phone rang. "Damn it," he said out loud as he put his drink down and walked to the ringing phone.

"Hello?" said Sam aggressively.

The person on the other end of the call was Sam's grandpa, Vic. Sam and his grandpa were close, so it wasn't that odd that he called, but what was odd was that he sounded panicked like Sam had never heard him before.

"Sam, something's wrong and I need you to come over here right now!" Victor said on the other end of the line.

"What is it?" asked Sam.

"Just get here as soon as you can," replied Vic before hanging up.

Sam was a twenty-four-year old bachelor who had spent his entire life in Ashbelle. The day high school ended, Sam walked over to the Ashbelle Company, got hired, and had been working there ever since. He had a bit of a reputation around town as a drunk and as a bully. He had gotten in trouble off and on all throughout high school, but never anything serious enough to land him in jail. He had once been a decent athlete, but his attitude and trouble making had gotten him kicked off more than one team.

Sam slammed the phone down, grabbed his keys, and ran to his car. He was slightly irritated that Grandpa Vic was taking him away from the game, but he figured he could calm his grandpa down once he got there and he could catch it over there. Sam lived on the south side of town near the company, so it was only about a three-minute drive to his grandpa's house.

When Sam pulled up at his Vic's house, which was located across the street from the tennis courts near the school, he saw his grandpa standing at the large front window staring at something. Besides the odd staring, Sam knew something was up as his grandpa was usually seated in his recliner watching TV whenever he came over. The house was one of the few houses with a view of the tennis courts, as the school was on the edge of town with not many houses around it.

Sam put his truck in park, got out, and rushed up to the house.

"About time you showed up!" snapped Victor as he opened the door and moved quickly back to in front of the window.

"Nice to see you, too, Grandpa. What's going on? I expected you to be on the ground hurt or something by how you were on the phone," said a confused Sam.

"Sam, I have to tell you something that I've never told anyone, not even your grandma or your dad," said Victor as he was still staring out the window at the tennis courts.

"Okay, what is it?" asked Sam.

Sam listened in awe as Victor proceeded to rapidly tell him the story of what had happened all those years ago with the bomb, the tunnel, the police officer, and so forth.

"Holy shit, Grandpa. Why, why are you telling me all of this now?" asked Sam in disbelief.

"Because I need you to do me a huge favor," Vic replied.

"Sure, Gramps, what…whatever you need," sputtered Sam.

"I need you to get your ass in that tunnel and bring the body back here. Can you do that for me?" said Vic in a hurried tone.

"Whoa, are you serious? Why now? Why not leave it there forever?" asked Sam.

"Because last night, Sam, I saw what I had hoped I would never see. Last night, four boys finally discovered the tunnel and went inside. I watched until they came out and left, and I just know they're going to go to the police soon and spill the beans. If the police find that body, I'm done for."

"Grandpa, relax. Even if they find that body, how on earth would they suspect you?" asked Sam.

"Because, boy, the night that it all went down, as we were moving our asses to get out of the tunnel, I dropped my ten-year service pin from Ashbelle. I begged the guys to let me go back and get it, but they said no way, and that damn older brother of Earl's threatened to shoot me, too, if I went back to get it."

"But Grandpa, lots of guys have ten-year service pins from Ashbelle. Not like there'd be DNA or anything on it," replied Sam.

"Boy, pull your head out of your ass. Each of those pins has the guy's name engraved on it. That pin puts me right by that body!" snapped Vic again.

"All right, all right, I'll do it. Show me where the entrance is," said Sam.

Vic spent the next minute or so describing to Sam where the entrance door was located.

As Sam ran out the front door with a flashlight in his hand, he couldn't believe what he was about to do. He had just learned in the last ten minutes that his grandpa, who was always a bit of a hardass, was involved in some serious shit and that he was now being asked to steal a body from a tunnel that no one in this town knew existed, and to bring it back to his grandpa's house—all in a rush and without being seen.

Trying to push all that aside, Sam darted across the street, across the tennis courts, and about halfway up the hill. Even with the flashlight, it was pretty dark, so he had a hard time finding the spot where the tunnel was, but after a minute or so, even though there was no sign of a door, he saw a little loose dirt and figured that had to be it. He never would've seen it if his grandpa hadn't described its exact location to him, as those kids had done such a good job covering it back up. His grandpa had told him not to leave the door exposed when he was done, but he was in such a rush that he ripped the well-constructed cover-up off the doorway and hurriedly tried to rip the door open.

Sam began to panic as he realized the door had no handle. *How the hell am I supposed to open this thing?* he thought to himself. *I'm screwed if those kids show back up with the police.* Finally, after what seemed like minutes, but was actually about forty-five seconds, Sam saw the hole in the door that the boys had made. Remembering the wheel on the inside of the door that his grandpa had told him would be there, he stuck his arm in to it and, although barely able to grab the wheel, he managed to and was able to spin it enough to open the door.

Now that he was in, he really felt rushed. His heart was beating a thousand times a minute and he was already sweating. He shut the door the best he could and shined his flashlight down the tunnel. As he moved in further, he told himself that he had to hurry, but he found it hard, as this place was dark, dank, and a tomb for a body that he was supposed to steal. "Pull yourself together, Sam," he told himself, just as his father and grandfather always said.

After what felt like forever, Sam found the body. It didn't look like he expected. He thought there'd be blood and guts everywhere like in the movies, but it was just a skeleton at this point. Although it was just a skeleton, Wilskie looked almost dignified, like a fallen soldier in his uniform with his badge still with a hint of shine left on it.

Not sure what to do next, Sam instinctively scooped up the body with both hands. Sam was a pretty big guy, so carrying the body out wasn't all that difficult for him. As he was about to run out, Sam quickly put the skeleton down and shined his light all over to try to find the service pin. He searched and searched, knowing the whole time that the clock was ticking, and right as he was about to give up, he finally saw it. He quickly scooped up the dusty pin, shoved it in his pocket, and re-scooped up Wilskie's skeleton and ran as fast as he could down the tunnel.

As Sam came to the doorway, he thought he heard talking, but decided it was just in his head.

Sam pushed the door open just enough to get his head out, and after not seeing or hearing any one, he exited the tunnel and laid the body on the ground and quickly put back as much dirt as he could to make it look like it did before; it didn't, but he didn't have any more time to waste on it. Thankfully for him, it was a dark night so he scooped the body back up and took off for his grandpa's house, hoping like mad that there weren't any dog walkers or late-night joggers out that he failed to see. As he reached Vic's house, he went down the driveway, took a left at the detached, one-car garage, and reentered the house from the back door in to the kitchen. He laid the body down quickly and sat down breathing heavily and not believing what he had just done. A minute later, he looked up and saw his grandpa staring at the skeleton.

After a minute of staring at Wilskie's remains, Vic looked at Sam and said, for the first time Sam could ever remember, "Great job, boy. Thank you. I love you."

"You too," said a dumbfounded Sam. Sam then reached in to his pocket, grabbed the pin, and held it out toward Vic.

"Is that...? You found the pin. I can't believe it. You've saved your old grandpa from spending the rest of his life in prison. I want you to know that I didn't want Wilskie to die, neither did my pal Earl—rest his soul. It was that crazy-ass brother of his that made that decision on his own and has caused me such anguish all these years, just waiting for someone to find out what happened. Did you know that that was why I bought this house and have never moved?" said Victor. "I've been watching that spot where the tunnel exits every day since 1944. I used to tell your Grandma— God rest her soul—that I never wanted to move because this was the perfect house for us. It wasn't, but she never argued."

"Wow, I'm sorry, Grandpa Vic. I had no idea," replied Sam.

"No one did. It's something I've lived with for over fifty years, and now it feels like a gigantic weight has been lifted," said Vic.

"At least now you don't have to worry any more," said Sam.

"I hope you're right. Now, let's get that body out of here. Scoop him up and follow me out to the garage, please," said Victor.

As they laid the skeleton on the garage floor, Sam said, "What now, Grandpa?"

"I want you to bury it here in the garage. I feel like that's the least I can do for poor Wilskie: to keep him here and give him some kind of burial. I know that sounds weird, but it's like we've been connected since that day all those years ago and it just seems like the right thing to do."

Sam spent the next hour digging a hole in the garage floor. The floor of the garage was concrete, but it was heavily cracked and therefore not difficult to pry up several pieces without making much noise. After an hour or so, Sam had dug a hole sufficiently sized to toss Wilskie in and cover him with some of the dirt he had dug out. After filling the hole back in and replacing the concrete pieces, it looked pretty much like it did before. Sam tossed the shovel into the pile of dirt remaining and went back in to the house, where he found his grandpa sitting at the kitchen table looking at an old photograph.

"Who's that, Grandpa?" asked Sam.

"That's my buddy Earl," Vic replied. "As horrible as that day was, it brought us even closer together and boy, do I miss that son of a bitch. He was the best friend I ever had. We used to do so much together; this picture was taken at his hunting land up north. He loved it up there and always invited your mother and me."

As Sam was about to walk out to his car to leave, Vic looked at him and said, "I'm sorry for bringing you in to this, Sam."

"It's okay, Grandpa. Talk to you soon," replied Sam as Victor shut the door and turned off the lights.

Chapter Eight

1944

Earl and Victor's work area on the Ashbelle Company factory floor was pretty much in the middle. It was a great place to work because from there you could see the whole floor and get a sense of what was going on in the factory. It was amazing how much drama and gossip went on in a factory full of tough guys.

Although working in the center was ideal, it was especially now as it allowed Earl and Vic a great view of the northwest corner where the bombs were kept in neatly stacked lines waiting to be loaded on to military trucks that came to the factory regularly.

Today, Earl was having a hard time focusing on his work because he was trying to think of a reason, any reason, to go over by the bombs. He didn't really have a good reason to be in that area, much less nosing around over there. The guys over there had gone through an extra security check and they were supposed to be the only ones who handled the bombs, but occasionally they needed extra help and that rule got overlooked. He kept hearing his brother in his head saying, *Find out a way to get your ass over there and get in that closet.* Earl knew that time was of the essence, as his brother kept reminding him, but he just couldn't find the opportunity or excuse to be over there. He was about to say "screw it" and just walk over there and claim to be lost or something when an opportunity finally presented itself.

Next thing Earl knew, a loud, terrible sound came from the loading dock area.

"Ahhhh! My foot! My foot!" screamed one of the guys who helped load the bombs on the military trucks.

"Oh shit!" said one of his co-workers. "You all right, man?"

The poor loader, who looked all of about thirty years old, had lost his grip and dropped one end of a bomb on his foot, and looked like he had probably broken it by the way he was screaming. His supervisor came running over and asked him if he was all right, and told him to go to the on-site clinic and get it looked at to see if it was broken; he also told the guy's co-worker to help him get there.

"I need two men to help load these up!" shouted the supervisor.

Earl turned and looked at the loading dock area and as quick as he could without looking too anxious, jogged over to the loading dock and said to the supervisor, "My buddy and I can help out."

The supervisor, although clearly upset that one of his men may have just broken his foot and would be out for a while, said to Earl, "Okay, thanks. This whole row goes on this truck. Be careful. And if any one asks, you're okay to be over here. I'll back in a little bit. I'm heading to the clinic to check on him if anyone's looking for me."

"Will do, sir," replied Earl. Earl quickly ran over to get Vic.

"Vic, get your ass over here. We're loading bombs today," said Earl with a smile on his face.

"Great," replied Victor in a very sarcastic tone until he realized what that meant. "Oh, I see. Better get over there, then, shouldn't we?"

Earl and Vic hurried back over to the loading dock and set up to start loading bombs on to one of the several military trucks waiting in line.

After they began to load a bomb on to the cart, Earl looked for his opportunity to get in to the closet. He knew he didn't have much time before the supervisor made his way back; he would probably be paying extra attention to them. Fortunately, the other workers weren't paying all that much attention to Earl and Victor. They were a tight-knit group over here, always joking around and pulling each other's chain. Basically, they couldn't care less about the two fill-ins. This allowed Earl to slowly sneak over to the door labeled "Janitor's Closet" as Victor kept working.

Earl moved slowly but determinedly the twenty or so feet to the door labeled "JC"; he kept looking around, but no one seemed to be paying him any attention. Once he reached the closet, Earl sat there for a second shaking his head, unable to fathom that this plain, ugly door led to the entrance to this big, top-secret tunnel system—that is, if the map Lenny had gotten his hands on was legit.

Earl looked at the door, the clock ticking in his head, and was shocked to see that all that was keeping the door sealed was a tiny lock that a child could easily cut through. Earl looked around again to make sure no one was paying any attention to him as he pulled out the shears he always had on his work belt and cut the lock right off while laughing to himself about the abysmal security that was in place for something like this. But then again, why draw attention with a huge lock?

After snapping out of it, Earl opened the door just enough to sneak in closing the door behind him. Once inside, he took the flashlight off of his work belt and turned it on. To his dismay, he saw exactly what you think you'd see in a janitor's closet: mops, brooms, some chemicals.

Damn, Earl thought to himself. Lenny's map was totally wrong. Maybe this whole tunnel system didn't really exist after all.

Just as he was about to sneak back out, he accidentally kicked a broom, which fell to the back wall. "Shit," Earl said to himself, hoping that wasn't so loud as to draw attention to the closet. But then something hit him: The sound of the broom hitting the back wall didn't sound like he thought it would; it sounded like it had hit something metal even though the other walls of the room were concrete. Confused, he quickly moved stuff out of the way blocking his view of the back wall and saw something very strange: a big circular wheel, like those you see on a bank vault.

There's no reason a janitor's closet would have that, he thought to himself.

Next, Earl grabbed the wheel and tried to turn it. At first it wouldn't budge and Earl thought of something that Lenny had said to him once while recalling a story of how he stole something from a safe: "Most safes won't open right away, they're designed to slow possible robbers down; the key is to put some weight in to it, that helps line up the gears inside." So that's what Earl did the second time and, sure enough, Earl heard bolts release and the whole back wall opened to a cavernous, concrete area slowly angling downward away from the factory. He couldn't believe it; he'd found the entrance!

Knowing that he had been in there a while, he quickly pulled the door shut, mistakenly spinning the wheel in to the lock position, and exited the closet. After taking a quick look around and seeing that no one seemed to be paying any attention to him, he quickly ran to catch up with Victor.

"What the hell took you so long?" said Vic in an angry whisper. "The supervisor came back and wondered where you were. I told him that you probably ran off to the bathroom."

"Sorry, good thinking on that bathroom excuse. Vic, I found the entrance to the tunnel," whispered Earl.

"You serious?" asked Victor in amazement.

"You bet your ass I did. Now we just need to figure out a way to get one of these bombs out of here and we're rich, buddy!" replied Earl while trying not to show his excitement.

"Keep your voice down, you moron," said Vic as he indiscreetly shook Earl's hand.

The rest of the workday dragged on for Earl, as he couldn't wait to tell Lenny about his finding the tunnel entrance. Once the 5:00 whistle blew, he grabbed Victor and said, "Let's go!" and they trucked out of the factory in as fast of a walking pace as they could.

Chapter Nine

1997

"I still can't stop thinking about it, man," said Chris to Andrew as the between class bell rang.

"I know. Me neither. It doesn't make any sense," replied Andrew.

"We have to go back. We have to see if we can find anything that might give us a clue as to where that body might have gone. Someone took that guy. They must've been watching us the whole time," said Chris.

"Even if they were, and they went in after we left, and they came across the skeleton, why would they steal the body? You think they'd have freaked out and ran away," said Andrew.

"Maybe they knew it was in there all along," replied Chris.

"Maybe," said Andrew as he looked up and saw Tanner and Trev walking up to them.

"What's up, boys?" said Tanner.

"Chris and I are going back to the hillside tonight to see if we missed anything," said Andrew.

"Yeah, you guys in?" asked Chris.

Both Trev and Tanner nodded yes.

"All right, let's all meet by the tennis courts tonight at 10:00. It'll be dark then. Also, don't park close or it'll look suspicious," said Andrew.

◄o►

That night, Tanner, Trevor, and Andrew ended up driving together to the tennis courts; Chris had called the guys earlier saying he'd meet them on the hill. The three of them parked and headed to the tunnel exit. Once they were at the top of the hill, they saw Chris sitting on the hillside with a strange look on his face.

Tanner jokingly said, "What's wrong, bro? You look like weirder than normal."

Chris hushed them and then signaled for them to come down by him. "Dude, what's up?" whispered Trev.

"Don't look, but there is an old man in a house across the street staring at us right now."

Of course, all the guys instinctively turned around and scanned the area. Seeing no one, Andrew, Trev, and Tanner all turned back around, but Chris kept staring at something across the street over the tennis courts.

"Dude, which house are you looking at?" asked Tanner.

"Guys, there is a man in that brick house across the tennis courts staring at us right now. You don't see him?" said Chris anxiously.

The three other boys looked again, but saw nothing.

"I think you're paranoid, man." said Tanner. "I don't see anyone. How could you? It's pitch black out here."

"You see that big front window? He was just there watching us, I swear!" said Chris.

"Okay, maybe you did see someone, but he was probably just looking out his window. An old man couldn't see us from there at this time of night," replied Andrew.

"No, man, he was looking right at me and then at us," replied Chris.

"Dude, let it go. Old people are always looking out their windows, keeping an eye on things. Don't let your imagination run wild," replied Trev.

"Whatever, man. I know what I saw. That old man knows something, I can feel it!" replied Chris.

"Dude, Trev's right," said Tanner. "Old people are always looking out their windows, and it makes sense he'd be looking right at four high schoolers sitting on the hill by school at 10:00 at night."

"He knows something, but whatever," said Chris.

After discussing what to do for another ten minutes or so, the guys decided that it'd be too risky to tear the ground up and head inside again, so they left and headed home.

As the guys were leaving—three in Andrew's Chevy Blazer and Chris on his bike—Andrew rolled down his window and said, "Go home. Don't do anything stupid."

Chris just waved and took off, fortunately in the direction of his house.

As they drove away, Trev said to Tanner and Andrew, "He's going to do something stupid."

"I know. He's not going to let it go," replied Tanner.

Sam pulled up at his grandfather's house after work; he wasn't terribly surprised that his grandpa had called him that morning before work, asking him to come over when he was done. Sam figured he was probably still freaked out over what had gone down the other night.

"C'mon in, Sam. Thanks for coming over," said Victor as he answered the door.

"No problem, Grandpa. Everything all right?" asked Sam.

"Yeah, but we might have a problem," replied Victor.

"There's no problem, Grandpa. We talked about this the other night. No one saw me, and it's all taken care of," replied Sam.

"No, listen to me. Last night, right as I was about to head up to bed, I saw that those boys who found the tunnel were back and looking it over," snapped Vic.

"Were they with the police or no?" asked Sam.

"No police," replied Vic.

"It makes sense that they'd come back. They're probably freaked out and confused about what happened the other night, too. I don't see why them coming back is a problem," said Sam, trying to calm his grandpa down.

"Well, the thing is, as I was standing in front of the window watching them, one of them looked directly at me and just stared at me like he knew I was involved or something," said Vic.

"You're just being paranoid, Grandpa. Why would he have any reason whatsoever to suspect you of anything? He probably thought you were just some neighbor checking out a group of boys hanging around after dark," replied Sam.

"You're probably right, but I don't know. It felt weird," agreed Vic as he sat down in his recliner.

"I'll tell you what, I'm here now, why don't we have some dinner and drinks and see if they show up again tonight?" said Sam as he patted his grandpa on the shoulder.

"That'd be great, thank you," said Vic in an exhausted tone.

"Don't do it, Chris. That's a terrible idea," said Andrew as he and Chris were walking out of school on a Friday afternoon.

"I have to, man. The way he was looking at us, he knows something," replied Chris.

"No, it's like I said the other night, he just saw a group of teenagers standing around at night and was checking us out to see if were up to something or not," said Andrew.

"I hear you, but I saw him. You guys didn't. He had this look on his face, not like he was just curious, but like he didn't like us by that tunnel, like he knew it was there and was worried about it."

"That's a lot to read from a face across the street, behind a window, in the dark, wouldn't you say?"

"I know it sounds crazy, but I'm still going over there to talk to him."

"Again, terrible idea, but do it if you want. Let me know how it goes."

"Sounds good. Later," said Chris as he walked toward the bike rack.

"Aren't you ever going to get your driver's license?" yelled Andrew.

"Why would I? I've got this sweet bike and all you guys to drive me around," answered Chris with a big smile on his face.

◄O►

"So my boss says to me, 'Sam, if that's how you feel about it, why don't you just quit?' I hate the guy, Grandpa. I'd love to punch him in the throat," said Sam as he and Victor were finishing up their dinner at the kitchen table.

"I've heard you complain about your boss a lot, Sam. Can't you try to get transferred to a different part of the factory or something?" replied Victor.

"I'm working on it," said Sam as he finished another beer.

Just then, the doorbell rang. Victor didn't get many visitors, so as he rose from the kitchen table, he said, "Probably just someone trying to sell something."

As Victor approached the door, he checked the front window like he always did to see who it was, this way he could decide whether to answer or not. As he checked this time, he took a step back and almost fell backward. "Sam, get in here, quick!"

Hopping up and afraid his grandpa had fallen or something, Sam ran toward the front window and said, "What's wrong, Grandpa? Are you all right?"

"I'm fine, but the boy who saw me the other night from by the tunnel, he's here! At the door!" said Vic in a surprisingly panicky voice.

"Okay, okay, even if he's here to ask you about the tunnel, just deny you know anything about it," replied Sam, trying to settle his grandpa down.

"All right," said Victor as he approached the door.

As the door opened up, Chris's immediate thought besides *I should never have come here*, was how helpless this little old man looked. Nothing like someone who would have anything to do with a murder or some secret tunnel. "Hello sir, my name is Chris—"

"What do you want?" snapped Vic.

Taken aback, Chris stammered, "I...I was wondering if I could ask you a question."

"About what?" snapped Vic again. "I don't like people, especially not snot-nosed teenagers, coming over here bothering me!"

Trying to compose himself, Chris said, "I'm sorry for bothering you, but I'm just wondering if you saw me and a couple of my friends over by the tennis courts the other night?"

"As a matter of fact I did! I was just keeping an eye on things. So what?" replied Victor defensively.

"Sir, I didn't come here to upset you. I just was wondering if I could ask you a few questions," replied Chris.

Just then, Sam came to the door and calmly said, "Hi, I'm his grandson. Come on in."

"What the hell are you doing, Sam? I don't want this..." said Vic, looking at Sam like he was crazy.

Cutting him off, Sam said, "Sorry, my grandpa is a little irritable today. Come on in and have a seat."

"Ah, okay, thanks," said Chris as he slid by Sam, who reeked of alcohol.

"So, what do you want to ask my grandpa about?" said Sam in a bit of slurred speech.

"Well, I just...it seemed the other night that when you were looking at me and my group of friends that you seemed, I don't know, concerned."

"Of course I was concerned. There was a group of four teenage boys hanging around at night near the school," said Victor.

Sam cut in again and said, "What he means, Chris, is that seeing four boys just hanging out that time of night can make someone concerned, not knowing what they're up to."

"And that makes total sense. It's just that…and I know this won't make sense, but it seemed like you were afraid we were going to find something," replied Chris.

"Find something? What the hell are you talking about, son? Find what?" said Victor, getting a little heated now.

"Nothing. I don't know. Is there something near that hill that you know about?"

"Okay, I've had just about enough of this. I'd like you to leave," said Vic, irritated.

"Just a minute, Grandpa," said Sam. "Let's let Chris here say what he has to say."

"Thanks," said Chris as he tried to focus on Sam and not the angry old man in the recliner. "I guess what I'm trying to say is, is there any reason why your grandpa wouldn't want people hanging around on that hillside?"

"I'm sorry, Chris, but can you just come out and say what it is you are getting at? Did you find something over there?" said Sam as he pointed toward the hill.

"No, I mean, nothing really. Just some weird stuff, that's all," said Chris, now feeling a little uneasy. "Maybe I should go."

"Like what kind of weird stuff?" said Sam as he sat forward in his seat, suddenly changing from the nice, somewhat intoxicated guy to a scary dude who might fly off the handle at any second.

"You know what, I shouldn't have come here. I'll just be going," said Chris, getting up from the couch he was sitting on.

All of a sudden, Sam popped up and put a hand on Chris' shoulder and said, "You're not going anywhere. Sit the hell down!"

Chris, now completely frightened, slid off the couch between Sam's legs, popped up, and started to move quickly toward the door when all of a sudden he hit the floor like a ton of bricks. The old man had held out his cane and tripped Chris, sending him flying to the floor.

"Nice try, but I don't think so. Now sit your ass back down!" yelled Sam as he moved to block the front door.

Chris sat back on the couch, staring at both Victor and Sam. He knew he needed to get out of that house, but he also knew that there was no way he could get through Sam, who appeared to be significantly taller and stronger than he was. "You guys can't kidnap me. My, ah, my parents know where I am."

"You know what, Chris? I just don't believe you," said Vic. "Now I've got some questions for you."

Chris was panicking now, looking from Sam to Victor, wondering what his next move should be when the old man said to him, "If you found what I think you found, then I'm afraid I can't let you leave here."

"Please sir, we didn't find anything," said a scared Chris.

"Bullshit!" yelled the old man. "You found a door in that hill, didn't you?"

"I knew it!" Chris fired back. "You were watching us the whole time and you knew about that tunnel. Who's the dead body that was inside?"

"That, my friend, was an Ashbelle police officer who showed up in the wrong place at the wrong time," replied Victor.

"So you took the body knowing we were going to go to the police. What did you do with him?" asked Chris.

"Let's just say Officer Wilskie has been moved to a closer resting place. Don't worry, you'll get to see him again when you join him. Sam, my boy, why don't you escort Chris here to the garage and do what needs to be done," said Vic in a surprisingly calm voice.

"You sure about this, Grandpa?" asked Sam.

That gave Chris a glimmer of hope. The old man was obviously crazy, but was the grandson dumb enough to kill him? Chris thought to himself. Maybe. The grandson looked crazy, too, and was clearly intoxicated…and that gave Chris an idea.

Chris knew if he just made a run for it out the back of the house, Sam was going to catch him; he didn't know the layout of the house or where the back door even was, and Sam obviously did. Sam also looked pretty athletic and fast, so he had to think of something else. Looking to his left, he saw a pretty full glass of what appeared to be whiskey or bourbon. He quickly grabbed it, popped up, and threw it in Sam's face. Sam reached his hands to his eyes to stop the burning of the alcohol and that's when Chris popped up quickly and shoved Sam as hard as he could, knocking him backward in to the front door. Sam yelped, and Chris dashed out of the room and toward the back of the house. As he was nearing the old man, Vic stuck out his cane again, but this time Chris jumped over it and continued toward the back of the house. He saw a light on up ahead and assumed that this was the kitchen. This house appeared to have relatively the same layout as many in the Village where the back door was off of the kitchen. Even with that being the case, these 1920s homes in Ashbelle were all closed concept and maze-like. As he was trying to get around the table in the crowded dining room, he looked behind him and saw Sam fast on his heels, yelling at him to stop. Chris finally got through the dining room and spotted the kitchen to his right. As he looked back again to check on Sam, he felt a huge pain in his right thigh. He had run directly in to a heavy, expensive-looking chess table that he hadn't seen and he rolled over it as it tipped over to the floor, spilling its pieces everywhere. Just then he looked back and saw Sam dive at him and get a firm grip on his ankle.

"Got you now, you little shit!" yelled Sam.

Chris quickly reached over and grabbed the biggest chess piece he could get his hands on and threw it straight at Sam's face. The chess piece hit Sam square in the nose and Sam immediately grabbed his nose in an attempt to stop the blood that was now gushing from it, thereby releasing his grip on Chris's ankle.

"You broke my nose, you son of a bitch!" yelled Sam.

Sensing his freedom, Chris got up and ran for the kitchen. Just as he entered the kitchen and saw the back door, he looked back again to see where Sam was; Sam was on his feet, but moving very slowly as he still held his nose. Chris smiled and turned to run out when he saw something coming at him from above.

As Chris and Sam had been fighting, Vic had gotten up and taken the other route to the kitchen through the office, where he had picked up a baseball bat and was waiting for Chris in the kitchen. As he saw Chris enter the kitchen, he stepped forward and brought the bat down on his forehead as hard as he could. Chris instantly fell backward on to the floor, dead.

Sam entered the kitchen, still holding his nose, and looked at Chris, motionless on the floor with blood oozing out of his forehead. He then, in disbelief, looked at his grandpa; Vic was standing there with his old Louisville Slugger at his side, staring down and Chris.

Without even looking up, Vic said, "I don't know what he knew and what he didn't know, but unfortunately Christopher made a mistake coming here tonight. I am not going to prison at this age for a murder that happened fifty years ago. He should've just minded his own business."

Not sure what to say, and now snapped in to being stone sober, Sam replied, "Okay, Grandpa, whatever you say, but now what?"

Victor slowly sat down in his favorite kitchen chair, laid the bat on the floor, and said, "Bury him in the garage next to Wilskie. I guess they're both part of the same story now."

Chapter Ten

1944

As Lenny sat behind the school waiting for Earl and Victor to arrive, he thought about all the good times he had had at the school and the various sports fields he could see as he leaned on his car. Lenny had enjoyed school, not because he liked the actual learning part but because it had been a blast for him. He had been a pretty good athlete (football, baseball, basketball), had done pretty well with the girls, and had a really good group of friends—anyone would've said he was pretty popular.

He had plans after high school. He never wanted to work at Ashbelle like many guys in the town; he was going to join the Navy and see the world. That plan went awry after he moved to Milwaukee after high school and started running with a rough crowd. Eventually he got in to selling and using drugs and began committing stupid crimes. He knew it was wrong, but he was a boneheaded eighteen-year old who thought he was smart and invincible. Eventually he had agreed to take part in a gas station robbery, which, long story short, had cost him five years of his life in prison.

Just as he started to relive that stupid robbery in his head, he saw Earl and Victor walking toward him and snapped back to reality.

"Hey boys, how was working in that dark, dirty factory today?" Lenny asked sarcastically.

"Whatever, Lenny, listen, I've got some good news," said Earl as he recounted the whole story of how he had found the entrance to the tunnel.

"Seriously? You better not be messing with me," replied Lenny.

"Lenny, it's true, I swear it. I can't believe it either," said Earl with a look on his face that Vic had never seen before in all the years he knew him. It was the look of making his big brother proud of him. Vic had a feeling that that hadn't happened much in Earl's life.

"Nice job, little brother. That's great. I wish I'd had the same luck," replied Lenny. "I went to the spot where the map said to and there's nothing there but grass and trees—no doorways, drains, grates, nothing. C'mon, I'll show you."

Lenny grabbed the map and the three men walked over to the spot on the hill where the tunnel exit should be according to the map.

"It should be right here," said Lenny, pointing at the spot on the map.

This area was one that Earl and Lenny were familiar with; they had learned to play tennis on these courts as kids. The two side-by-side tennis courts were located in a depression in the ground that dipped down with hills on both sides, and the hill closest to the school was significantly bigger than the hill closest to the road. This gave passersby, including police, a great view of the hillside; there was some cover on the hillside if one were trying to stay out of view, some pretty decent sized trees here and there, but it was mostly open. Fortunately for the three guys, the area wasn't frequently driven by or walked by, as it was adjacent to the north end of the town. There were some houses that faced the hillside, but very few.

Lenny stood about halfway up the hill and said, "This is where it should be. Look here." He pointed at a rectangle on the map indicating where the tunnel exit should be.

"Damn, you're right, Lenny. There's nothing here but grass and trees. What the hell?" said a frustrated Earl.

"Does the map say anything else? Like how the one of the factory floor said 'J.C.'?" asked Victor.

"No, nothing at all," said Lenny with his head dipped and his hands on his hips.

"Well, this is just great! I risk my butt at work today to actually find that entrance and we can't find what should be the easier one!" said Earl.

"Relax, bud, we'll find it," said Victor.

"Love your optimism," replied a resigned Earl, "but I just don't know."

"Boo hoo. You two babies need to stop talking so much and keep looking," snapped Lenny as he searched.

"Up yours, Lenny. Why don't you shut up?" yelled Earl.

"Why don't you make me?" replied Lenny.

"I will!" said Earl as he reached down, picked up a rock, and threw it straight at Lenny's head. Lenny ducked as the rock whizzed by his head and in to the hill behind him.

"Is that all you've got?" yelled Lenny.

"That's it! You're dead!" replied Earl.

As the two brothers were about to go at it, Victor suddenly snapped, "Both of you shut up for a second! Did you guys hear that?"

"Hear what?" replied Earl.

"Throw another rock," said Victor with a smile on his face.

"Don't do it, bro!" yelled Lenny.

"Not at you, Lenny," said Vic. "Move out of the way. Earl, throw it again in the same direction."

"Fine," said Earl as he grabbed another rock, wound up, and threw it in the same direction. This time, as it hit the hill, they all heard a very faint *clang* as the rock went in to the hill further than one would've thought it would have.

"What the hell?" asked Earl as they all ran toward where the rock had hit.

Lenny elbowed Earl in the stomach to slow him down and got there first. He immediately started digging with his hands in to the small hole where the rock had gone in to the hill. After a few minutes, he had dug out enough dirt where he could reach his hand a little ways in to the hill.

"Hand me a stick, Earl," he said.

Earl quickly picked up one and handed it to Lenny. Lenny reached in to the hole and stabbed with the stick and there was the *clang* again.

"Holy shit, there's definitely something metal back there!" said an excited Lenny. They had found the tunnel exit.

All three of the men just stood up and looked at each other in astonishment.

"I can't believe it," said Earl.

Victor sat there with his hands on his head and said, "It's genius. Build it in to the side of the hill where no one will really walk over it and you really don't have to conceal it with much other than some earth."

"And if it weren't for my cat-like speed, we never would've found it," said Lenny with a smirk on his face.

Chapter Eleven

1997

"Hello?" said a groggy Andrew as the phone rang at seven on Saturday morning. "No, he's not here…He never came home last night? Did you check with Trev or Tanner? I'll see what I can find out and let you know. Okay, bye."

"Who's calling so damn early on a weekend?" shouted Andrew's dad from the other room.

"Chris's mom. She's all worried because he didn't come home last night," replied Andrew.

"Probably passed out on someone's couch," his dad yelled back.

Andrew rolled back over to go back to sleep when his eyes popped open and he shot up in bed. "Shit!" he said to himself, remembering that Chris was going to that old man's house by the tennis courts after school yesterday.

Last night, he, Tanner, Trev, and some other kids from their class had been partying while sitting around a fire on Trev's deck. Chris was supposed to show up, but he never did. Everyone just assumed that he was with some girl and that he'd show up later. When Andrew had left Trev's last night, he was going to stop by Chris's house to see if he was there to see what he had been up to all night, but it was late and he didn't want to risk waking anyone up. *I'll talk to him tomorrow*, Andrew thought as he drove past Chris's house on his way home.

Andrew quickly threw on some clothes, grabbed a Pop Tart, and drove to the police station.

Once he was there, he tried to walk right in to Chief Preston's office after seeing him sitting in his chair through the office window.

"Whoa, whoa, Andrew. I can't just let you walk in there. The chief is on an important phone call at the moment," said Sharon.

"It can't wait. I need to see him right now," said Andrew irritatingly.

"I told you, he's busy right now. You'll just have to wait," Sharon replied.

"The hell with that!" said Andrew as he jumped the half wall and threw open Chief Preston's door.

"I'm so sorry, Chief Preston. I told him you were on an important phone call," said an exasperated Sharon.

Preston looked up and could tell from the look on Andrew's face that something was seriously wrong. "Let me call you back. Something's come up here."

"Thank you, Sharon, but it's okay. Please shut the door on your way out" said Preston.

After Sharon had reluctantly closed the door behind her, Preston looked at Andrew and said, "What's wrong? Sit down."

"Did Chris's parents call you yet?" asked Andrew as he paced back and forth.

"No, why? What's going on?" asked Preston. "Sit down and let's talk about this calmly."

Andrew plopped on the couch and said, "Well, his mom called me this morning freaking out because he didn't come home last night."

"Okay, okay. Well, a couple of things before we jump to conclusions here. First off, Chris is a high schooler who enjoys some beers now and then. Maybe he's passed out on someone's couch. Secondly, until someone's been missing for twenty-four hours, we don't list them as a missing person," replied Preston, trying to calm Andrew down.

"I mean, it's possible, but it's just that Chris didn't show up to a party last night and we all just assumed he was with some girl, but then it hit me this morning after his mom called that he told me he was going somewhere after school yesterday and I'm worried it didn't go well," said Andrew.

"Where was he going?" asked Preston.

"I tried to talk him out of it; I told him it was a stupid idea," said Andrew.

Preston leaned forward, put his hands on Andrew's shoulders and said, "Listen to me. Slow down and tell me where he was going and why it was a bad idea."

"Okay, sorry. Well, the other night, we all met up by the tunnel exit just to talk about what the hell happened to that body. I know you think we made it up about there being a body, but there was one, I swear it."

"It's not that I think you made it up, son. It's just that without a body, I can't do anything," replied Preston. "Have you or your friends mentioned anything to anyone about the tunnel?"

"No, we've just kept it to ourselves, like you asked," replied Andrew.

"Good. We don't need that information out—at least until I hear back from the Feds. I've been in contact with them about it and they asked me to keep it a secret for now, too, so I appreciate you boys keeping it hush, hush," said Preston. "Now, go on. You were saying that Chris was going somewhere after school yesterday…"

"Yeah, so anyway, Chris told me yesterday at school that he was going to some old man's house that he swears was watching us suspiciously while we were by the tunnel," began Andrew. "I told him, even though none of us other than him saw the old man looking out his window at us, that it wasn't weird even if he did. I mean, four teenagers hanging out at night, that's reason for suspicion. Anyway, he couldn't let it go. He kept saying something about how the way the old man was looking, not like he was just keeping an eye out, but that he seemed scared or worried or something, like he was worried we had found something or something like that. I told Chris that he was reading way too much in to it, but he told me he was going over there to ask the old man some questions to see if he knew anything about the tunnel and the body inside."

"So you're worried that Chris went to this old gentleman's house and what, that something happened to him there?" asked Preston.

"I don't know. I just thought I should tell you," replied Andrew.

Preston didn't want to discount Andrew's concern, so he gently leaned back and calmly said to Andrew, "Tell you what, let's give Chris some time to show up. It's a Saturday and it's still pretty early. He's probably not even awake yet. If he doesn't show up or contact his parents by day's end, we'll look in to it further. And, if need be, maybe we'll go have a talk with this older guy. Sound good, Andrew?"

"I guess. Thanks, Chief. I'm probably overreacting, but it just doesn't feel right," replied Andrew.

"Thanks for coming to me with it," replied Preston as Andrew left his office and the police station.

◀◦▶

"Yes ma'am...I know it's scary, but Chris is a...please, try to remain calm...We'll find him...Talk soon." said Preston as he hung up the phone with Chris's mom. Preston leaned back in his chair and exhaled, trying not to think the worst. Based on his discussion earlier in the day with Andrew, Preston feared the worst, but kept telling himself that Andrew and Chris were both kids and sometimes kids jump to conclusions and sometimes kids don't come home for a few days. He'd seen it happen before in Ashbelle and it had always ended up that someone was mad at their parents for something and wanted to "show them" by freaking them out for a few days.

Preston spent the next couple of hours tracking down Andrew, Tanner, and Trev to see if any of them knew where Chris was or had talked to him; the fact that all three didn't know and hadn't talked to him yet today was not good. Contrary to popular belief, teenage boys need their friends as badly and talk to them as frequently as teenage girls, and the fact that Chris hadn't been seen by or in contact with any of his three best friends meant that something was very wrong.

Preston was about to pull out of Andrew's driveway to go back to the station when he stopped and said, in a hushed voice so that Andrew's dad, who was on the front steps, couldn't hear, "Can you meet me in front of the school at 10:00?"

"Sure, why? Have you got any news on Chris?"

"Unfortunately not, but I know what we need to do next and I need your help with it."

"Okay, I'll be there."

"Thanks Andrew."

—◄o►—

As Andrew pulled up to the front of the school, he saw Preston leaning against his squad car with a flashlight in his hand. "Hey Chief, what's going on?"

"I need you to show me which house you think Chris went to visit," replied Preston. "If we head to the tunnel exit, do you think you can show me which house it is?" asked Preston.

"Pretty sure. There's not too many houses nearby, but they all do kind of look alike," said Andrew.

"Here, grab this flashlight, but don't use it when we get close. I don't want to arouse any suspicion," said Preston as he began walking toward the tunnel exit.

On the walk there, Preston wanted to put Andrew at ease, so he recounted a story about how he and some of his friends had once, with tremendous effort, managed to get a half barrel of beer up on top of the school.

"No way! Those are super heavy…or, ah, so I've heard," said Andrew.

"Riiight, so you've heard. Anyways, those things are about 160 pounds full," laughed Preston.

"How did you guys manage that?" asked Andrew as they continued walking through the parking lot behind the school.

"Well, when I was a senior, like you are now, the drinking age was eighteen, so having the half barrel wasn't illegal, so getting it wasn't, but how we got it up on top of the school was a different story. We had these two guys in our class, identical twins name Tim and Tom Schmidt. These guys were known as the twin towers. They were both about six foot six inches and built— not like some of the tall guys you see who are wafer thin and gangly. Anyways, there was a group of about eight of us and six of us would climb up to the next landing and put our arms down to grab the barrel that the Schmidt brothers were somehow able to lift above their heads easily. The rest of us struggled to get the barrel up to the next level each time, but those two just kept lifting it at every level all the way to the top like it was nothing. Let's just say that we drained that thing that night up there and then, foolishly, climbed down. Can't believe no one fell."

"Was it hard to climb down with the barrel?" asked Andrew.

"Well, I hate to admit it and don't you boys ever do this, but the Schmidt brothers tossed it from the top of the school right in to the courtyard in front of the school and that thing bounced so high— couldn't believe it—and then, it rolled right on to School Street and hit a parked car. Man, we were idiots. Good times, though," laughed Preston.

As they neared the hill, Preston signaled for quiet and they cut the flashlights and proceeded down the hill to where the tunnel exit was.

Looking across the street toward the houses across from the tennis court, Preston said to Andrew, "So, can you remember which house Chris said had the old man staring at him?"

Andrew said, "I didn't see the old man, none of us did, but I now remember Chris saying it was a house that had the big front window in the front."

"Okay," replied Preston, "but I need you to be sure, because I can't just go up to three or four houses asking about a missing kid."

"I'm sure. Chris said it was that one on the end."

"Okay," said Preston with a bit of a concerned look on his face. "That's Victor's house. My father knew him back in the day when they both worked at the Ashbelle Company; he's lived in that house for over fifty years. He's cranky at times, but he seems harmless. He does have a bit of a pain-in-the-ass grandson, though; used to get in trouble a lot around here. I'm going to go pay Victor a visit. You can go home now. Thanks for meeting me here."

"I want to go with you," replied Andrew.

"Can't, Andrew. I'm sorry. Official police business. Why don't you go home and get some sleep? I'll call you if I get any answers."

"All right, goodnight, Chief," said a dismayed Andrew as he climbed the hill and began to walk to his car. As he reached the top of the hill, he turned around and saw Preston crossing the tennis courts. He noticed Preston had his hand on his pistol and began to wonder if perhaps Preston knew more than he was telling him.

As Andrew was about to get in his car, he said, "Forget this," turned around and began heading toward this Victor's house. "I've got to look around myself. Chris would do it for me," he said to himself.

As Preston neared Victor's house, he was thinking how best to approach the situation. He knew Victor, but not real well, and Victor was not known as the nicest person in the world; he probably wouldn't appreciate a visit from the police, especially at this time of night. Perhaps Victor was already watching him as he climbed the slight hill and crossed the street.

As Preston hit the front of Victor's yard, he spotted a vehicle parked in the driveway and hoped it wasn't Sam's, but assumed it was, as Victor probably didn't have too many visitors.

As he had told Andrew, Victor's grandson had a reputation around town as an angry drunk and an overall pain in the ass, and he really wasn't looking forward to dealing with him.

Preston reached the front step and rang the doorbell; he could see Victor and Sam watching TV through the large front window.

"Who the hell is that at this time?" said Victor.

"I don't know, Grandpa. I'll check," replied Sam as he got up to get the door. "Well, well, well, Chief Preston, so great to see you again," said Sam sarcastically.

"Sam, good to see you again. How's everything going?" asked Preston.

"Fine. What are you doing here?" asked Sam in a tone that let Preston know this wasn't going to be easy.

"I was hoping to have a word with your grandpa. May I come in?"

"Nah, I don't think so. No warrant, no entry!" snapped Sam as he was about to slam the door in Preston's face.

"Let him in, Sam, and stop being so rude to our gallant police chief. Come on in, David," said Victor from his recliner.

Sam did as he was told, but stared at Preston with the eyes of someone not only distrustful of the police, but also as someone who had had plenty of police show up at their door.

"Hello Victor, nice to see you again."

"Forgive me for not getting up. My knees don't work like they used to. How's your old man?"

"He's good. Mom and him retired to Texas a few years back. Couldn't stand the winters."

"Well tell him I said 'hi.' Now, what is it you wanted to talk about at this hour?"

Andrew tried to keep in the shadows, avoiding any light being cast by the beautiful, old, stone streetlights that were located throughout the Village. As he approached the house, he could see Preston inside the front room talking to what looked like an old man and a younger man, probably the grandson Preston had mentioned. He was thinking at this point that he probably should have gone home and let Preston handle it from here, but he couldn't. He had to see for himself.

The main thing Andrew was looking for was Chris's bike. Chris's mom had mentioned that he left on it the other night when they last saw him. When Andrew got to the sidewalk, he ducked low and started to make his way up the driveway. It was a typical driveway in Ashbelle, boulevard-style with a strip of grass running up the middle of two paved tire tracks toward a small, detached garage.

Andrew stayed low as he crept along the side of the house. He would take a few steps and stop again, knowing that there were several windows from which he could be spotted on the side of the house. Finally, he rounded the back of the house. He scanned the backyard to see if there was any sign of Chris's bike. If he could find it, he could prove that Chris had been here and that whatever bullshit story the old man and his grandson were telling the chief was a lie.

The backyard was dark. Thankfully he still had the flashlight Preston had given him before. He was glad that there was no motion light that would attract attention, but it meant that he did have to turn on the flash-light. He took a look in to a window at the back of the house, and not seeing anyone, he turned the flashlight on and began scanning the backyard. The backyard was nothing special; it had a small garden, a cracked concrete patio, and some old, dirty lawn chairs with a full ashtray between them.

After scanning the backyard and not seeing the bike leaned up against the house or lying in the backyard, Andrew turned and looked at the small, detached garage and saw the single, dirty window on the side wall facing him. He quietly made his way to the garage, turned on the flashlight, and attempted to look inside the garage. He was able to see inside a bit and un-fortunately, it looked normal enough. No sign of the bike. He was about to give up, but seeing how messy and cluttered the garage was, he thought that he had to get inside and look around to make sure the bike—or some-thing worse—wasn't in there.

After checking behind him once more and seeing no one, he tried to open the door but couldn't, as it was locked. The door looked as old as the house, so he knew that a good solid shoulder to it would break the frame and get him in, so he took one last look around and rammed his shoulder in to the door. Just as he suspected, it opened easily. Unfortunately, some paint cans that were located behind the door fell to the ground, making a noise that Andrew hoped hadn't been heard inside the house. He wanted to run, but he'd come this far and he knew he had to keep looking for Chris's bike.

Andrew quickly shut the door behind him and turned on his flashlight. There was a switch on the wall, but he couldn't risk turning it on. That would draw attention for sure, he thought.

As he scanned his flashlight around the garage, he was shocked to see how much junk there was. There clearly hadn't been a car parked in here in years. Old paint cans, piles of magazines, and oddly enough, a big pile of dirt. *Weird*, he thought to himself. After a few minutes with no luck, he was about to get out of there when he saw what appeared to be a tire sticking out from under an old, ratty blanket. Andrew made his way to the corner and lifted the blanket, exposing a black Trek mountain bike just the same as Chris's bike. He tried not to get too excited yet, though, as this was a bike you could find kids riding throughout the Village. To be absolutely sure it was Chris's bike, he had to check out the handlebars.

Andrew pulled the blanket completely off and saw what he dreaded seeing. In the middle of the handlebars, just above the front light, was a Pearl Jam sticker; the guys had gone to the see Pearl Jam play last year in Milwaukee and Chris had bought a sticker, which he put on his bike, right between the handlebars.

"Those sons of bitches," Andrew said to himself. They probably had Chris locked up in the basement or even worse, he thought. He was so angry, he wanted to storm through the front door of the house and tell Preston what he had found, but knowing that was stupid, he thought it'd be best to get the hell out of there and wait for Preston by his squad car.

Andrew began to make his way around the piles of junk and was a few feet from the door when he saw a large figure standing in the doorway staring at him.

"The hell do you think you're doing, boy?" said someone who Andrew assumed was the grandson.

"I was...just...ah..." stammered Andrew as he was searching for any excuse but finding none.

"Either you're a low-life criminal who's trying to steal from an elderly man's garage or you're looking for something in particular. Which is it, boy?" said Sam.

Andrew didn't know what to say, but instead was thinking of how best to get the hell out of the garage. To do that, he'd have to get by this pretty built guy blocking his only way out. Then it hit Andrew that this guy reeked of alcohol and looked unsteady on his feet.

Sam stuck his finger out and pointed at Andrew and said in a slurred speech, "Don't even think of trying to run, boy. I'll destroy you!"

The distance between Sam and Andrew was maybe about ten feet, and Andrew suddenly had an idea. With his hands raised, Andrew said, "Dude, I'm really sorry. You totally caught me. Please don't call the cops."

"Damn right I'm going to call the cops. Get over here," said Sam with a satisfied smirk on his face.

With his hands still raised, Andrew started to slowly walk toward Sam, saying, "I understand. I'd do the same thing."

Then suddenly Andrew ran at Sam, lowered his shoulder, and placed it square in Sam's chest. The hit caused the intoxicated, unsteady Sam to fly backward and hit the ground with enough force to knock the wind out of him. Andrew knew it was time to run, but felt like he needed to get the bike to show Preston if he wanted the chief to believe him. He took a quick look at Sam and, seeing that he was holding his chest and rolling back and forth on the ground in pain, Andrew kicked him hard in the ribs and ran back in to the garage; he looked for a garage door opener on the wall so he could get the bike out easily, but didn't see one. "Seriously?" he said to himself. Next, he went to the garage door, unlocked it manually, and slid it up before turning back in to grab the bike. As he was trying to get the bike out of the garage, he saw Sam running at him.

"You're going to pay for that!" snarled Sam.

Bike in hand, but realizing he couldn't get on it and start pedaling away before Sam got to him, Andrew pulled out the flashlight, shone it right in Sam's eyes, and, knowing that Sam was temporarily blinded and disoriented, ran up to him and kicked him square in the groin. Sam fell like a ton of bricks, grabbing the injured area and moaning in pain.

"Take that, bitch!" said Andrew as he hopped on the bike and drove away as fast as he could toward Preston's squad car.

Chapter Twelve
1944

The next day after work, Vic and Earl walked across the street to the Clydesdale—the English pub located in the Patriot Club—to meet Lenny. As they walked in the front door and were descending the stairs in to the pub, Vic looked at Earl and said, "Didn't your brother get kicked out of here or something?"

"Oh yeah, he got in to it with some guy from out of town one night. They were both drunk, of course. Anyway, the guy called him something and Lenny busted a beer bottle over the guy's head. Guy was out cold with a huge cut on his head, bleeding all over. The guys Lenny was with got him out of there before the police could arrive, and the other guy's buddies did the same thing with him, so no charges were ever filed, but the Clydesdale banned him for a year," replied Earl.

"That must have been a while ago, huh?" asked Vic.

"Not really. A few Christmases ago. I'm surprised they ever let him back in. Oh, there he is," said Earl, pointing to a booth near the back.

As they reached the table, Lenny had two cold beers waiting for them and said, "This round's on me, seeing as you guys did such a great job with you know what."

"Thanks, Lenny," said Earl. "I think the hardest part is yet to come, though."

"Definitely," replied a less-than-enthusiastic Vic.

"You're always such a downer, man," replied Lenny.

"Okay guys, let's talk about the next step," said Earl, trying to be the peacemaker.

"You're right," said Lenny as he slammed what remained of his beer. "Hey sweetheart, another beer, please!"

"So what's the plan, Lenny?" asked Earl.

"It's simple…" began Lenny before Vic jumped in.

"Yeah, right."

"There he goes again, Earl. How is this guy your best friend?" asked Lenny while pointing at Vic.

"Okay, okay, can we just talk about the plan, guys?" said a frustrated Earl.

"Fine, so here's what I'm thinking," said Lenny before pausing for a second while the waitress brought him his beer. She put the beer down on the table in front of Lenny and he, of course, slapped her on the butt as she walked away.

"Nice, Lenny," said Earl sarcastically.

"She's loves me," he replied. "Anyways, so the beauty of finding both ends of the tunnel is that we don't even have to consider breaking in to the factory after hours to steal the thing. We can just enter through the tunnel exit and walk right in to the factory—assuming, of course, that you, Earl, can get back in that closet and leave the door open a crack for us. Why again did you lock the door after opening it last time?"

"He was just trying to leave it as he found it. Any one else would've done the same thing. Not his fault," replied Victor.

"Whatever. What's done is done. Now, it's about getting that door back open," replied Lenny.

"Oh man," said Earl, scratching his head. "Not sure how I can get back in there again, but I'll think of something. Any ideas, Vic?"

"Yeah, any ideas, smart guy?" said Lenny.

"Actually yeah," replied Vic.

"Great, let's hear it," said Earl.

"Okay, I know a guy—Timmy Smythe. You know who he is, right, Earl?" asked Vic.

Earl nodded his head and said, "The young kid straight off the boat from Ireland, right?"

"Right," Victor replied. "So Timmy owes me about $100 from a poker game a while back.

"Whoa!" said Earl. "He's already that deep in gambling debt?"

"Yeah, and that's just to me. Who knows who else he owes money to," replied Vic. "Anyways, I'm going to tell him that if he can 'accidentally' drop a bomb on his foot like the guy did the day you and I had to step in, Earl, they'll ask for guys to come fill in while he goes to the clinic to get it looked at. I'll tell him that his debt is gone if he can do that."

"Okay, good, but how do we make sure that we are the two guys picked to fill in?" asked Earl.

"Well, I figure if we give him a certain time to have his 'accident,' then we can make sure we're the first ones to run to the scene and offer to fill in. The supervisor will say sure to not waste any time, plus he knows we've done it before so he won't have to show us how to do it," said Vic.

"I hate to say it, but that's a good plan," replied Lenny before letting out a disgusting burp.

"You are ridiculous!" said Earl as he shook his head in disgust at Lenny. "Vic, good plan. What do we do if the guy who's going to have the 'accident' asks you why you are willing to waive his debt to get him to do that?" asked Earl.

"I'll tell him that part of the deal is he can't ask any questions or tell a soul about it," replied Vic. "I'll also mention that if he does, your brother here will pay him a visit when he least expects it and will make it a painful one."

"Nice, Vic," laughed Lenny. "Now you're talking."

"Okay, so we've got that covered. Now how do we get in to the tunnel from the exit?" asked Earl.

"I've got that all taken care of," said Lenny. "While I was in prison, I met a guy who was in for safe-cracking, and he knew how to crack any lock.

So he and I became good friends and he taught me everything he knew. After I got out of prison, him and I did a job together and he let me do the locks, so I'm pretty sure I'll be able to get the door at the tunnel exit open."

"And what if you can't?" chimed Vic.

"Well, then plan B."

"Which is?" asked Earl.

"Well then, we'll have to break in to the factory. Even if it comes to that, the good news is we'd just have to break in, not try to get back out with the bomb because we know we can take it out through the tunnel and open the door from the inside if it comes to that," replied Lenny.

"I hope it doesn't come to that. There's like five or six guards walking around the place all night. It'd be hard to not be seen," said Earl with a worried look on his face.

"Assuming we can get in the factory via the tunnel by the tennis courts, what's the plan once we get the bomb out of the tunnel?" asked Vic.

"I've got a guy who will be waiting with a truck and a trailer. He'll roll up, we'll put it on there, and he'll take off. Easy as that," replied Lenny as he finished another beer.

Earl, looking nervous, said to the table, "Okay. Sounds good. Next question is when are we thinking of doing this?"

"Well, my buyer is very anxious, so the sooner the better," replied Lenny. "Vic, when can you talk to your guy who owes you money?"

"He actually lives here at the Patriot Club. I don't see him in here, so I'm guessing he's up in his room. I'll go pay him a visit right now," said Victor.

"Good. Let's meet back here after work tomorrow," said Lenny. "Sweetheart, another round!"

Victor stood up from the table and said, "All right, I'm out of here. Off to talk to Timmy."

"All right. Goodnight Vic. See you tomorrow morning." said Earl as the waitress put another round of beers on the table.

—◄o►—

As Victor left the Clydesdale, he climbed the brick stairs and headed across the building to the lobby where he asked the clerk what room Timmy's was. After he got the room number and some directions, he left the lobby and headed up a flight of stairs near the front desk. On his way to Timmy's room, he saw men playing pool and cards in one room and other men taking a class of some sort in another room. This place would have been fun to live in if he were single, he thought. It looked like the men of the Ashbelle Company played hard as well as worked hard.

As he reached Timmy's door, he was a little nervous. He had never done anything like this before, and he felt uncomfortable with it. Steeling himself, he took a deep breath and knocked on the door.

"Who the hell is it?" shouted Timmy from inside.

"It's Vic from work. Open the damned door," replied Vic, trying to sound tough.

Timmy opened the door and nervously said, "Aye, Vic...Listen, friend, I don't have your money. I'm sorry. That's what you're here for, right?"

In another attempt to look tough, Vic bumped shoulders with Timmy as he walked past him and entered the room.

"Pretty nice place you got here," said Vic after looking around.

"Yeah, they treat us well and don't charge a ton either," replied Timmy.

"Timmy, have a seat. I've got some good news for you," said Vic, pointing at a chair by a small desk.

Timmy sat down as he was told and said, "Good news, great."

"I'm willing to waive that $100 you owe me if you can do me a small favor," said Vic.

"Wow, that'd be great. What favor do you need?" asked a still-nervous Timmy.

"I need you to get hurt at work," said Vic.

"I don't understand." replied Timmy.

"Tomorrow at work at exactly 1:15, as you are loading up the Army truck that always arrives at 1:00, you are going to drop a bomb on your foot and you are going to scream like bloody hell that your foot is broken," said Vic, pointing at Timmy.

"Why would you want me to hurt myself on purpose?" asked a confused Timmy.

"My reason is of no concern to you," replied Vic.

"If I do that, I'll be out of work for months. Worth much more than $100," said Timmy as he shook his head back and forth.

"Well, if you're smart, you are going to miss your foot and let it hit only your toes. That way you'll only be out a couple of days. Guys work with broken toes all the time at the factory," replied Vic.

"I don't know," said Timmy looking at the ground.

"Well, listen, Timmy, I like you, I really do, but if you don't do this or if I find out you've told anyone at all, broken toes are only going to be the beginning of your injuries. Do I make myself clear?" asked Vic.

"Okay, okay, I'll do it," said a clearly shaken Timmy.

Victor took a few steps toward the door, patted Timmy on the back, and said, "Good decision, Timmy, and, hey, now you don't have to keep avoiding me at work as you won't owe me any money. Have a goodnight, son," said Vic as he walked out the door, shutting it behind him.

Vic took a few steps and then let out a long sigh of relief. He was glad that was over and that soon this whole thing would be done with. He was sick of this world of crime and sneaking around and just wanted life to go back to the way it was—except with a ton more money, he kept telling himself.

◄○►

It was noon the following day at the factory. Lunchtime. The bell had just rung and all the men put down their tools and were reaching for their lunchboxes. Vic and Earl grabbed theirs and sat down to eat with the other guys who worked in their area. As they sat leaning up against a machine, Vic whispered to Earl, "It goes down today, 1:15."

Earl almost choked on his sandwich before whispering back, "So soon?"

"My meeting with Timmy went as planned last night and knowing your brother was getting anxious, I just said it," whispered Vic. "I also didn't want to give Timmy time to think about it."

"Okay," said Earl as he took a bite of his sandwich. "We better be ready then. Lenny will be happy."

Vic stood up and looked across the floor toward the bomb-loading area. He saw Timmy Smythe staring back at him. Both men nodded and then looked away.

At 1:00, an Army truck pulled up to the loading bay on time just as it always did. Victor gave Earl a look as if to say "be ready." The next fifteen minutes were agonizing for Earl. He knew it had to happen, but he wasn't looking forward to it. He knew what he had to do and he didn't want to let down his best friend or his brother. Tick tock, the time seemed to be dragging by. Earl was trying to do some work to make the time go by faster, but it was no use. He just found himself staring at the clock.

"No use staring at the clock, Earl," said one of his co-workers. "Ain't going to make the day any shorter."

"Yeah," Earl replied trying to look cool and collected. He could feel Victor staring at him and beads of sweat began to collect on his forehead.

Keep it together, Earl. Don't freak out now, Vic thought to himself. Victor looked up and saw the clock hit 1:15. He gave Earl one last look and then came the *bang* of a bomb hitting the ground, followed by the painful scream of Timmy Smythe, "My foot, my foot! Damn that hurts!"

Victor took off running toward Timmy, feigning both surprise and concern for Timmy's well-being. "You all right, Timmy?" he said as he reached him. The supervisor came over and said, "Damn it, Smythe! Get yourself to the clinic. You two men, help Timmy to the clinic ASAP! Hey Vic, can you and Earl help out again?" he asked.

"No problem, I feel so badly for Timmy." Vic replied, shaking his head.

"Yeah, me too," said Earl as he looked over Vic's shoulder.

"Thanks. I've seen this before. That poor bastard's foot is probably broken. I may need you guys for a week or more. I'll talk to your supervisor to clear it," replied the obviously frustrated supervisor.

"Anything to help out," said Victor, trying to suppress a smile.

"All right, everyone. Back to work. Nothing to see here," yelled the supervisor before storming off.

"That couldn't have worked out any better," said Earl.

"Yep. Step one down," replied Vic. "Now for step two, you have to get back in to that closet and leave that door open. Keep an eye out for any opportunities."

"Right, will do," replied Earl.

Earl and Vic got right to work loading bombs on to the carts and helping load them on to the Army trucks that came and went the rest of the day.

Around mid-afternoon, Earl was getting anxious to get back in the closet and said, "Vic, the supervisor looks distracted. I'm going."

"Don't you dare. He's not distracted. He's just talking to a guy," whispered Vic in an admonishing tone.

But by the time he was done saying it, Earl had already started to make his way over to the closet. He was about five feet away from it when the supervisor yelled, "Hey, Earl, you lost or something? Get back over here. Break time isn't for fifteen more minutes!"

Damn it, Vic thought to himself.

Earl just laughed and threw his hands up in the air, but Victor knew that Earl was too anxious and needed to play it cool, because although the supervisor liked them, he wouldn't hesitate to replace them if they weren't keeping up with the rest of the loading crew.

"You need to calm down. An opportunity will present itself, but don't force it," said Victor to Earl as he got back.

"Sorry Vic, you're right," replied Earl, looking at the ground like a kid who had just been scolded.

"Listen, I get it, but we have to do this the right way to not arouse suspicion. Now come on, help me load this thing," replied Vic while patting Earl on the shoulder.

◄○►

After work, Earl and Vic walked back in to the Clydesdale to meet Lenny like they had planned. As they reached the table, they saw several bottles of beer around Lenny and the waitress sitting on his lap, laughing at some stupid joke he had just told her.

"Ah, here's Tweedle-Dee and Tweedle-Dum. Time to get back to work, sweetheart," said Lenny as the they sat down at the table.

"She's a nice girl, Lenny. Don't screw her over," said Earl.

"Ah, I'm just having some fun," said Lenny. "So, any news to tell me?"

"Actually, yes," replied Vic in a clearly annoyed tone. "Last night I went to visit Timmy and he did exactly as we discussed."

"Good," said Lenny cutting him off, "so when's he going to do it?"

"Well, as I was saying, I kind of surprised myself and told him it had to be today at work."

"Today? Awesome. Did he do it or do I need to pay Timmy a visit?" replied Lenny, once again cutting Vic off.

"I'll tell you, just stop interrupting me," said a clearly miffed Vic.

"Sorry, Mr. Sensitive. Go on," said Lenny before taking a big drink.

"Whatever. Anyway, so yes, he did do it and it actually worked out perfectly. Your brother and I have a reason to be in that area for at least the next week."

"And I'm going to find an opportunity to get back in to that closet and get that door open," replied Earl.

"Perfect. Good boys," replied Lenny disparagingly.

◄○►

The next two days came and went at work with no opportunity for Earl to get in to the closet, and both men were starting to think it wasn't going to happen. However, their luck changed the next day.

It was about an hour after lunch and Earl and Vic were doing what they were supposed to be doing when suddenly they heard a groan from the supervisor. Vic looked over and saw the supervisor bent over with his hands hugging his stomach and looking quite pale. "You all right there?" asked Vic.

The supervisor looked at Vic and barely got out, "No, I think I ate something rotten and I feel like I'm going to…" before running from the factory floor to the bathroom.

All the loaders and many others watched the whole thing transpire, which led to a mixture of concern and laughter. Guys were chatting and laughing with each other when Vic looked at Earl and said, "Now, go!"

Earl turned and walked steadily toward the closet, trying not to draw attention; none of the loaders or other workers were even watching him as they were either discussing what had just happened or kept on working.

As Earl reached the door, he noticed that the lock that he had cut off the first time he went in to the closet had not been replaced; then again, why should it? No one ever used this door, so no one would notice a missing lock. Earl opened the door as little as possible and slid in. Knowing what to do this time, he moved quickly, got to the wheel, turned it, and opened the door in to the tunnel. He only left it open a little and put all the junk back in front of it just in case somebody would come in. A few minutes after entering the closet, he was out and back by Vic's side.

"It's done, Vic. It's flipping done!" said an excited Earl.

"Well done, buddy, but keep your voice down and act normally. We don't need anyone suspecting anything," replied Vic.

◄○►

That night, after work, all three men once again met up at the Clydesdale. As usual, Lenny was already there when Vic and Earl arrived and appeared to be on his fourth or fifth whiskey.

The two sat down and Lenny could tell right away from the look on Earl's face that there was good news.

"I could tell from the minute you two came down the stairs that you had something good to tell me; you had that goofy grin on your face, brother, that you always had as a kid when you were excited," said Lenny before Vic and Earl could even sit down. "So tell me, what's up?"

"Lenny, it's done," said Earl, a little too loudly drawing stares from nearby tables.

"Okay, keep it down a little and tell me exactly what's done," said Lenny.

"The opportunity finally presented itself that allowed me to sneak in to the janitor's closet and open the door," said Earl, trying to keep his voice down.

"That is awesome, brother! Great job! Put her here" replied Lenny, holding out his hand for Earl to shake.

"Thanks," said Earl with a grin on his face, belying the fact that his brother rarely complimented him.

"Okay boys, so now that we don't have to break in to the factory, I suppose it doesn't matter what night we do this thing," said Lenny.

"That's true, but we're going to have to make sure whatever night we do it to be super quiet, though. Security is super tight these days ever since we started making stuff for the war. They doubled nightly security around the exterior of the factory," said Vic.

"We can do that," replied a confident Lenny while taking down another whiskey.

"Well, not as easy to do that as you think, big brother. Moving those heavy carts and bombs around is actually pretty loud," replied Earl.

"I've got an idea," said Victor.

"What's that, bud?" said Earl.

"Tomorrow night is the monthly union meeting, right?" said Vic.

"Yeah, so what?" said Lenny, clearly not understanding what Victor was getting at.

"Those union meetings are really just excuses for the boys to get drunk and loud, right?" replied Vic.

"True, that's what makes them fun," said Earl, smiling and nodding his head.

Victor continued, "With the union hall being right next to the factory, the guards will assume that any noise they hear is coming from the hall. That'll give us the cover we need."

Lenny thought about it for a second and then said, "I like it. Nice thinking, Victor."

"Wait, did you just compliment me?" asked Victor in a sarcastic tone.

"I guess I did. Don't get used to it!" said Lenny. "Okay, so how many guards are around the building at night?"

"Five most nights, but union meeting nights, maybe another two or three," said Vic.

"The good news is, they're all on the perimeter. They only come in if they hear something suspicious," said Earl.

"How can you be sure there won't be one inside the factory?" asked Lenny.

"Vic and I bowl with one of the guards and he told us so," replied Earl.

"Okay, tomorrow night it is. My buyer will be very happy to hear that," said Lenny.

"Okay, but how about the other door? How are we going to get in the exit door by the tennis courts?" asked Earl.

"Well, I think it's fair to assume that the tunnel exit door has the same lock mechanism as the one in the janitor's closet, so a tool I can get my hands on should make us able to turn the wheel from the outside," said Lenny

"Yeah, but is that tool something loud like a drill or something?" asked Earl.

"Easy, boys. It just so happens that I have a little bit of experience in opening those from the other side," said Lenny with a laugh. "And the best part is, it won't be loud at all. You guys just leave that part up to me."

"Another 'skill' you picked up in prison, Lenny?" asked Earl, shaking his head.

"Rehabilitation, brother. Rehabilitation." answered Lenny with a big belly laugh.

Chapter Thirteen
1997

As Preston left Victor's house, he heard the door slam behind him. He knew he had made Victor angry tonight, questioning him about a missing kid. It was understandable. Vic told him that the kid did come to his house, but after hearing what he had to say, he slammed the door on the kid and told him to get off his property. He then said that he hadn't seen or heard from him since. It was a plausible story; Vic was a grumpy old man, and that's what a grumpy old man would do.

Preston was just about to his squad car, thinking how he was going to tell Chris's parents that he had not come any closer to finding their son, when he saw Andrew leaning up against his car.

"I thought you were going home, Andrew. What's up?"

"Chief, I don't even know where to begin, but I followed you to the old man's house tonight and I know for a fact Chris was there!"

"He was. The old man told me so."

"Wait, what?"

"Yeah, he said Chris knocked on the door, asked him some strange questions, and then he told him to get the hell off his property."

"Well, he lied to you."

"What do you mean? What makes you say that?"

"Well, for starters, this is Chris's bike."

"Andrew, there's a lot of bikes like that around the Village."

"True, but not with this Pearl Jam sticker on the front handlebars!"

"How did you get the bike?"

Andrew recounted the whole story to Preston about seeing the bike, breaking in to the garage, and his run-in with Sam.

"Well, that explains the grandson disappearing during my little talk with Victor."

"Yeah."

After asking Andrew if he was all right, Preston said, "What was that you said you saw in the garage besides the bike?"

"Just piles of junk."

"No, you mentioned something about dirt?"

"Oh yeah, there was a pile of dirt, which I thought was strange. I mean, who keeps a pile of dirt in their garage?" said Andrew.

"How did the floor of the garage look?" asked Preston.

"Pretty beat up. Cracked concrete mostly, but it was pretty dark so I couldn't see most of it. Why?" asked Andrew.

"I need to get in to that garage," said a visibly upset Preston.

"But I got the bike, Chief. Isn't that good enough?"

"It's not quite enough, but it will help a lot because that old crank won't be able to explain why he has Chris's bike and that's going to give me what I need to get a search warrant," replied Preston while putting his hand on Andrew's shoulder.

"Good," said Andrew.

"I don't know how to say this, but I'm worried that maybe Chris is still in that garage," said Preston, looking at the ground.

"No, he's not. I would've seen him if he were tied up in there or something. Maybe they have him the basement or in a room upstairs or something," said Andrew frantically.

Preston put both hands on Andrew's shoulders, looked him in the eye, and said, "Andrew, look at me son."

"Okay, I am," said a confused Andrew.

"I mean, I'm afraid that Chris might be buried in the garage. Do you understand what I'm saying?" said Preston.

Andrew looked at Preston confused, and then suddenly he got what Preston meant. "No, no way. I can't believe it. Chris dead? There's no way."

"I hope to God I'm wrong, Andrew, but I need to get in to that garage," replied Preston.

—◄o►—

The next morning, Victor was awoken by a loud knocking on his door. He sat up in bed and yelled, "Hold on, hold on, I'm coming." As he made his way down the stairs, he saw out the front window that it was Chief Preston.

As he reached the bottom of the stairs, Victor sighed to himself and then threw the front door open. "I told you not to come back here!"

"I'd like to say that I'm sorry to bother you again, Victor, but I'm not because you and I need to have another talk," replied Preston.

"Not right now. I'm going back to bed. Come back when you have a warrant!" said Victor as he attempted to slam the door in Preston's face.

Preston took a step forward and stopped the slamming door in its tracks and said, "Victor, I'm not asking."

"Then talk," said Victor with his arms crossed in the middle of the doorway, making it perfectly clear he wasn't about to let Preston inside.

"Okay, I have reason to believe that when the young man we discussed last night came to your house to ask you questions, that you didn't just tell him to get off your property. I think something else went down that night," replied Preston as he took a step closer to Victor, forcing Victor to retreat slightly.

"I don't know what you mean. I told you what happened," said Victor.

"Mind if I come inside and take a look around?" asked Preston.

"Not a chance in hell," replied Victor as he shoved his finger in Preston's face.

"Okay, I'll just come back with a warrant, then," replied Preston as he turned to walk away from the house.

"Wait a second. What do you want to see?" said a taken aback Victor.

"I want to see if there's anything that shows me that Chris came inside of your house—and possibly that he never left."

"Are you suggesting that…that I kidnapped him?" asked Victor, trying to sound innocent and feeble.

"Maybe…or maybe you killed him," replied Preston.

"Listen here, you smug son of a bitch, do you think I'm capable at this age of kidnapping or killing a teenage boy? Look at me!" said an angry Victor.

"No, not you, but that grandson of yours is perfectly capable of both. You said that he was here with you when Chris came over that night."

"Well, yeah, but like I said, Sam was inside while I talked to the kid at the door."

"I know you said that, but do you mind explaining to me how Chris's bike ended up in your garage?"

"Wait a second, how the hell do you know what's in my garage? Wait a damned second, are you believing the word of that thief that Sam had to deal with last night?"

"That thief was a friend of Chris's, who, I admit, shouldn't have broken in to your garage, but the question still stands. How the hell did Chris's bike get in your garage?" asked Preston.

"I…I have no idea. Are you really going to believe a thieving teenage punk over me?"

"Well, at this point, yeah, I guess I am," replied Preston.

"I'm going to have you fired for this harassment of me. I know most everyone on the Village Board!"

"You're welcome to try, Victor. Now, how about you try to answer my question," said Preston.

"Well, that's ah, simple…See, that kid who came here, came on his bike, but he left it when I told him to scram. I guess he was scared or something and just left without it. I told Sam to grab it and put it in the garage to teach that kid a lesson. I was going to give it back to him if he came back again."

"Right," said Preston. "Can I come in now?"

"Fine, I've got nothing to hide," replied an angry Victor.

"Is Sam here now?" asked Preston as he entered the house.

"No. He's at his place. Why?" replied Victor.

"Because I'd like to ask him some questions too," said Preston as he began to scan the front of the house.

Preston moved through the front room that contained the big front window and turned right to continue to look around while Victor continued to complain about this "harassment" from his lounger near the front window.

Preston crossed through the living room, through the dining room, and entered the kitchen. His plan was to immediately check the basement, as if Chris had been kidnapped, that seemed like the most likely place to look for him. He looked left and saw the basement steps, but on his way to them, he stopped dead in his tracks. A bright red stain on the carpet had caught his eye. The stained looked as though someone had unsuccessfully tried to clean it up. "Hey Victor, you a wine drinker?"

"No, wine's for sissies. I'm a beer and whiskey man," shouted Victor from the other room. "Why do you ask?"

"This stain in here on the floor in the kitchen. I was thinking maybe it was a wine stain, but based on what you just said, it can't be. How'd it get there?"

"Oh that, that's been there for years. My wife, God rest her soul, used to drink wine and that's where she accidentally dropped a bottle years ago."

"You know what kind of wine she dropped?" asked Preston as the stain looked more red than purple like most wine stains did.

"Um, no, but she liked Merlot," replied an annoyed Victor.

"Hmm, looks like somebody recently tried to clean it up," said Preston accusingly.

"Sam tried recently, but I told him it's never going to come up, I've tried before," replied Victor. "Are you done yet?"

Preston shook his head, knowing in his mind that the stain was Chris's blood. He wanted to bend down and cut a sample out of the rug, but he knew without a warrant that any evidence collected today could potentially be thrown out in a trial, so he proceeded to the basement.

After searching around the not-surprisingly messy basement, he was satisfied that there was nothing amiss. He came back up and told Victor he was heading out to the garage.

"Fine, hurry up!" yelled Victor.

Preston approached the detached garage and entered easily enough as the latch on the door was still broken from when Andrew had broken in. Preston flicked on the light and instantly saw the piles of stuff that took up most of the garage's shelves and floor. The garage was structurally sound, but had not held a vehicle for many, many years. Besides all the junk piles, was the pile of dirt that Andrew had mentioned. Preston was about to examine the dirt pile when he heard a voice from the doorway.

"Why the hell do you keep bothering my grandpa?"

"Sam, hi, how are you doing after your run-in with the robber last night?" said Preston, trying to not produce a smirk on his face.

"I'm fine. That little shit just caught me off-guard is all; he's lucky I'd had too much to drink or he'd be in a world of hurt right now," replied a clearly embarrassed Sam.

"I'm sure. Mind telling me what's the deal with this pile of dirt?"

"I think Grandpa had some guy bring it over so he could use it in his garden or something," replied Sam.

"Then why is it all the way in the back of the garage? Wouldn't it make sense to have it near the front so you could get to it easily?" asked Preston.

"I guess, man. I don't know," replied the obviously edgy Sam.

"Let me ask you this as well: Why is the concrete back here all broken up?"

"The concrete's broken up all over. It's an old garage, Preston," said Sam.

"True, but isn't it weird that this area over here is rectangular in shape rather than in random shapes like over the rest of the garage floor?" asked Preston.

"Listen, Chief, I don't know. I don't live here," replied Sam.

"Just seems like with this ground being all torn up and this dirt pile here, that someone's been digging here recently."

"What are you getting at?"

"I think that all of this plus the missing kid's bike makes me think that he was murdered here and buried under the garage!" yelled Preston.

"Yeah, well, I think you're wrong and that it's time you get the hell out of here before I call my grandpa's lawyer."

"Okay, okay, I'm leaving, but one last question for you. Any idea what that red stain on the carpet in the kitchen is from?"

"Don't even know what stain you're talking about," replied Sam, obviously lying.

"That's strange, because your grandpa said you tried to clean it up recently."

"Oh yeah, that stain. That's ah, that's from me. Yeah, I spilled Kool-Aid on it years ago."

"I see. All right, Sam. I'll talk to you soon. You can count on it," said Preston as he walked by Sam, forcing him to back up a few steps from the doorway.

"Better have a warrant next time you come back here! Stop harassing my grandpa!" yelled Sam as Preston walked down the driveway, painfully torn between believing that he had solved the missing case of Chris but also hoping to God that he was wrong.

When Preston got back to the police station, he knew he had to get a warrant ASAP because that dumbass Sam was going to get rid of the carpet, the dirt pile, and possibly attempt to lay fresh concrete over the newly disturbed section of floor in the garage. Preston called in an off-duty officer to keep an eye on Victor's house from down the street to look for anything suspicious.

◀◉▶

The next day, Chris's mom and stepfather came to the police department to meet with Preston to go over the latest developments in the search for Chris. At this point, the word was out that Chris was missing and the entire Village was being searched by hundreds of volunteers. Preston hoped and prayed that they'd find Chris alive, but knew in his heart that that was a very slim possibility.

"I am so sorry that you two are going through this right now. I can tell you that we are using every tool at our disposal to locate your son," said Preston to the couple as Chris's mom stared at him through eyes that had cried too much lately to have any tears left. "For legal reasons, I can't get in to all the details of the investigation, but I can tell you we have a very strong lead and I am in the process of getting a search warrant."

"For where?" asked Chris' stepfather.

"Like I said, I can't tell you that right now, but I should have it very soon and then I can give you more details," replied Preston.

"That's bullshit. This is our son. We want to know what you've got!" said Chris' stepfather angrily.

"I want to tell you everything, trust me, but if I tell you, whoever may be responsible for Chris's disappearance might be helped by me telling you. Does that make sense?" asked Preston.

"I guess," Chris' stepdad replied while gripping the arms of the chair so tight that Preston thought they both might break off.

"Is my son dead?" asked Chris's mom.

"Honestly, ma'am, I don't know. There's a chance that those search parties could find Chris dazed and confused or injured somewhere—that happens from time to time with missing person cases. I think it's a testament to you two and Chris that the Village has rallied so much to help out like it has," replied Preston.

Chris's parents stood up, thanked Preston, and left. Preston shut the door and window shades behind them and then, out of pure anger, picked up a baseball he kept on his desk and threw it as hard as he could against the wall. He wanted to string Vic and Sam up, and he felt an anger like he'd never felt before.

A few minutes later, his phone buzzed and he picked it up and said, "Not now, Sharon!" before sitting down in his desk chair with his hands on his head.

A minute later there was a knock at his office door. It was Sharon.

"Come in, Sharon. I'm sorry I yelled at you like that," said Preston, looking up at her.

"It's okay. I know you're going through a lot right now, but good news, your search warrant has been approved. Go get that old bastard." said Sharon as she began to walk out.

"Hold up, Sharon. Which old bastard are you referring to?" asked Preston, wondering how Sharon knew about Vic.

"Grumpy-pants Victor," she said.

"How do you know he's the target of the search warrant?" asked Preston, still confused as Sharon was never in the loop on details of open cases.

"I'm Sharon. Did you really think I wouldn't know?" asked Sharon with a big smirk on her face as she left the office.

Before Preston left to go pick up the warrant from the courthouse, he called the off-duty officer he had placed down the street from Victor's house and asked him if he'd seen anything going on. The officer said that a young, muscular guy had pulled away in a truck matching the description Preston had given him and that it looked like it was carrying dirt and rolled-up carpet.

That stupid son of a bitch, thought Preston. Now not only did he have his warrant, he now had a suspect disposing of evidence. Despite all that, Preston still did not have a murder weapon or a body. He knew he needed to find both to have a solid case—and to provide closure to Chris's family and friends.

Chapter Fourteen
1944

The next day at work was a very long one for Earl. He kept thinking that everyone around him knew what they were up to. He was so nervous, he dropped tools, broke some parts, and even got dizzy and had to sit down.

Victor came up to him as he was sitting and leaning up against the wall and whispered, "Listen, bud, I know you're nervous and you think everyone thinks you're up to something, but you're just letting your paranoia get to you. There's no reason for anyone to suspect anything out of the ordinary. Why don't you and I go outside for break today to get you some fresh air. How's that sound?"

"That sounds good. Thanks Vic. I know you're right. I just need to get this done and over with, you know?" replied Earl.

"I hear you, but losing control isn't going to help any. Besides, think of how much better you'll feel when you're counting your cash," said Victor smiling.

"That's true, pal. That's true," said Earl as Victor helped him up off the ground.

◄O►

Earl and Victor had both given lame excuses to miss tonight's union meeting. No one really cared. The meetings were basically always the same unless there were contract talks, which there weren't on tonight's agenda.

Lenny, Earl, and Victor had agreed to meet outside of town after work at the same place where they first went over the map. Earl and Vic pulled up and, as usual, Lenny was already there, but refreshingly, Vic didn't see any bottles or cans around him. As they pulled up, they got out and shook hands, and Victor was very pleased to see that Lenny appeared stone sober. Being a loud drunk tonight could make things go very badly.

"All right, boys, here's how it's going to go," said Lenny as the three of them stood there looking at each other with a combination of excitement and nervousness. "I want you both to go home and act like this is a normal Union meeting night: Eat dinner with your families and then head out just like you normally do at the same time you normally head out. Once you're clear of your house, change course and come meet me at the cemetery. No need to rush, as we have to wait until it gets dark to get started. Just make sure that you have a good story if anyone asks you what you're up to, why you're not going to the Union meeting, and so forth. Once it gets dark, we'll head to the hill and get started. We'll all take different routes as to avoid the suspicion that would come with three grown men walking together at nighttime on the edge of town. I've already stashed the items I need to get the door open in a bush near the tennis courts. Once we're in, we'll load up the bomb using the Union meeting's noise as cover; you've both mentioned that those meetings go well past midnight, so we shouldn't have to worry about it getting quiet while we're in there. We'll roll it all the way to the door in the hill and then you two will wait there while I sneak out to find my associate, who is going to be waiting a little ways from the school in his pickup and trailer. He and I will pull up next to the tennis courts. I'll let you guys know we're there, then we'll roll the bomb on to the trailer and then he's gone and he'll take care of the rest. Sound good? Make sense?"

"Sounds too easy, Lenny," said Earl nervously.

"Vic?" asked Lenny.

"I think that's a good plan. What do we do if something goes wrong, like the police drive by or there's a dog walker?" asked Victor.

"Shouldn't matter, as we'll only be exposed while rolling the bomb to the trailer, but if there is a problem, we'll have to deal with it," answered Lenny.

"What do you mean 'deal with it'?" asked Earl. "I don't want any one getting hurt."

"I'm not going to hurt any one. Do you think I'm some heartless monster?" asked Lenny all offended.

"No, I don't, it's just that, that…" stammered Earl.

"Listen, little brother, relax…We go in, we load up the bomb, we roll it out, load it up, and it's done. Easy," replied Lenny with his hands on Earl's shoulders. "This will all be over tonight and you guys can get back to your normal lives."

"If you say so, big brother," said Earl.

At approximately 6:15, both Earl and Victor kissed their wives good-bye and headed out their front doors, presumably on their way to the Union Hall. Victor lived near the Village's eight-way stop—a very out of place, oddly shaped intersection that required eight stop signs as so many roads collided there. It was laughable to Village residents because in a town as small as Ashbelle, no one could ever remember seeing more than three cars there at a single time, so it seemed wholly unnecessary. To walk from his house to the cemetery would normally only take about five minutes, but tonight, it would take a little longer as he would have to start off going the opposite way of the cemetery so his wife, or any other people who may see him, would assume he was heading to the Union Hall.

Once he had cleared a few blocks, he turned left at the school, went down another block, turned left again, and continued to the cemetery. He was now off of School Street, the main thoroughfare through town, which was the road he lived on, so he didn't think anyone would see him, but if they did, he was just going to say he forgot something at home and was going back to get it. If they asked why he didn't just head back the way he came, he didn't really have an answer; he'd just have to answer on the fly.

Fortunately he ran in to no one. He entered the cemetery, spotted Lenny by his car having a cigarette, and headed toward it, noticing that Earl had not yet arrived. He knew it would be awkward until Earl arrived, but he just shrugged his shoulders and continued on to Lenny.

"You ready for this, Vic?" asked Lenny in a somewhat condescending tone.

"Yep, are you?" replied Vic in an annoyed reply.

"You bet your ass I am. Excited to make some dough. I'm thinking about heading out to Las Vegas after this, try my luck," replied Lenny.

Victor was about to reply with some smart-aleck remark about how all Lenny would find out in Las Vegas was a way to lose all of his money when he saw Earl shuffling toward them.

"Hey buddy, you all right? You seem a little off," asked Victor.

"I'm fine. Just nervous is all," replied Earl.

"Stop being such a wuss, Earl. Man up. I need you sharp tonight, got it?" said Lenny as he flicked his cigarette at a gravestone.

"I'll be fine, Lenny. Can I have a cigarette?" said Earl to Lenny.

"Good idea. It'll help calm you down," replied Lenny as he handed Earl a smoke and lit up another one for himself. "We'll hang here for a couple of hours until it gets dark; if the police do come through here for some reason, we'll just say that we're here to visit a friend of mine who was killed in the war. That shouldn't raise any suspicions.

"You might want to come up with a name, though, Lenny," said Victor, "in case they ask whose gravesite you're visiting."

"Shut up, smart guy. Fine, I'll go find one," said Lenny as he walked off.

"I don't think your brother likes me, Earl," said Vic with a smile on his face.

"He's just not used to anyone talking to him like that; he likes to feel like he's the smartest and toughest guy in the room. Always has," replied Earl quietly so Lenny wouldn't hear him.

"Well, no offense, but the feeling is mutual," said Victor as he and Earl leaned on Lenny's car. "He's a loose cannon. I hope he doesn't screw this up tonight."

"Oh, here he comes. Let's talk about something else." replied Earl.

—◀○▶—

After a long and awkward couple of hours, darkness had set in and the men discussed the routes each would take to the hillside.

It was decided that Lenny would have the most direct route as that would get him there first so he could grab his tool bag out of the bush and get started on opening the door. Victor and Earl would have routes that took them to the hillside from different angles so they could see if there was anyone walking their dog or if the police were near.

As Victor approached the hill from behind the school, he was relieved, as he hadn't seen anyone on his way. As he reached the hillside, he carefully made his way down to the door where he saw that Lenny had already dug a portion of the hillside out using a shovel he had apparently had in his stashed tool bag.

"What the hell is that thing?" asked Vic as he neared the door.

"Holy crap you scared me!" replied Lenny, who was clearly not checking on his surroundings very well.

Vic was referring to the stethoscope-looking contraption around Lenny's neck.

"It's a safe-breaking tool," replied an annoyed Lenny as he placed the cup at the other end of the device on the door.

"I figured that, but how's that going to get us in there? There's no dial, just a wheel," asked Vic.

"An associate of mine in prison was a safe-cracker and he taught me all about it; wheels like this can have their gears realigned if you have a strong enough magnet, which this thing does," said Lenny as he moved the end of the contraption in small circles around the door.

"But how do you get the wheel to turn even if you can line the gears up from the outside?" asked Vic.

"Watch and learn, Mr. Smart Guy," said Lenny.

Vic was amazed as he heard a series of clicking sounds indicating that the gears were aligning.

"Okay, step one done. Now watch this," said Lenny as he moved the suction cup to the left and then did a slow clockwise motion upward. Victor couldn't believe it as he heard something moving from behind the door.

"Got it. I love this tool," said Lenny with a smile on his face. "Now I just have to pull."

Sure enough, the door opened a crack. Lenny had managed to open the metal door from the outside without making a hole in the door.

"Impressive," said Vic.

"I know. They're using these overseas to secretly break in to Nazi buildings apparently," said Lenny as he removed the plugs from his ears and smiled. "Where the hell is Earl?"

Earl was about two blocks from the tennis courts and was still very nervous but glad that he hadn't seen anyone out and about so far. "Almost there, almost there, just breathe," he kept telling himself. About thirty seconds later, Earl froze as he saw the lone Village police car rolling down School Street coming his way. *Damn it,* Earl thought to himself. "I'll look suspicious if I run or turn around," Earl said to himself as the police car got closer. Earl knew all of the Village police officers, so as the squad car pulled closer to him, he knew it was going to stop. Before he could fully gather himself, the police cruiser pulled over to the curb in front of him.

"Earl, buddy, how's it going?" said Officer James Wilskie out of his window as Earl reached the cruiser.

"Hey Jimmy," replied Earl.

"Surprised you're not at the Union Hall tonight. I just drove by and it sounds like a real serious meeting going on in there," said Wilskie sarcastically.

"Yeah, they can get pretty wild," said Earl as he was frantically searching his brain for an answer to the inevitable question that was about to come next.

"I thought you always attended those meetings. Not so tonight?" asked Wilskie in a confused, non-accusatory way.

"You're...you're right, I usually do go, but I didn't tonight because..." stumbled Victor as Wilskie looked at him confused. "I just didn't feel good as I was on my way to the meeting and I hoped that if I kept walking I might feel better," replied Earl, avoiding eye contact with Wilskie.

"You must have been walking for quite a while, Earl. The meeting started hours ago," said Wilskie.

"Oh, yeah, I mean I have been. All over the Village. The walking has helped. I think I'll just head to the meeting now.

Wilskie thought to himself that Earl was acting quite weird; not only would that be a ton of walking for hours straight, but if Earl was all over the Village, it seemed unlikely that Wilskie wouldn't have seen him at least once as he did his rounds throughout the Village.

"Sounds good. I'd be happy to give you a ride to the hall?"

"Ah, thanks, but I'm good," replied Earl as he forced a smile.

"All right, then. Have a good night, Earl, see you later," said Wilskie as he drove away.

Earl stood there for a second waving good-bye to Wilskie and then, as soon as he was out of sight, he turned quickly and basically ran to the hillside.

As Wilskie turned the corner, he was shaking his head at how weird Earl was acting; he knew Earl was a bit of a nervous guy, so it could be that he just had something on his mind or something was worrying him or whatever, but as Wilskie looked at his rearview mirror, he saw Earl turn and dash out of sight in the direction of the tennis courts, not toward the hall. "Very odd, but none of my business, I suppose."

As Earl arrived at the hillside, he said in a panting voice, "Hey guys, sorry. Jimmy Wilskie saw me walking and pulled up for a chat. He was wondering why I wasn't at the Union meeting and why I was on this side of town."

"So what'd you tell him?" asked Victor.

"Told him I didn't feel well and I was just trying to walk it off," replied Earl.

"Did he seem like he was suspicious?" asked Lenny.

"Don't think so. I've known Jimmy a long time. Don't see why he wouldn't believe me," said Earl.

"All right, you better be right," said Lenny with a menacing look. "So while you were dicking around, I got the door open. Now we're going to have to uncover the rest of it so we can get in. By the way, could you see us from the sidewalk?" asked Lenny.

"No, I couldn't. Probably why they built it here in the first place," replied Earl.

"Anyways, grab that other shovel and help us get this thing uncovered," said Lenny.

After a few minutes, the men had the door entirely uncovered. The door was painted camouflage. *Nice touch*, Vic thought.

Lenny reached his fingers in to the small crack that the door had opened and tried to pull it open enough for them to all get in.

"Shit!" said Lenny. "Earl, grab the crowbar out of my bag there."

Earl did as he said and handed the crowbar to Lenny, who shoved it in the crack; he was able to use it to open the door just enough so that he could get his fingers in far enough so he could open it and they could sneak in.

Once inside, Lenny turned back and snapped, "Earl, make sure it's pulled shut and bring the tools in, too!"

As the men turned on their flashlights and began down the dark corridor, they could hardly believe what they were doing. Not only were they in this supposedly fictitious tunnel system, they were entering the factory to commit treason.

Chapter Fifteen
1944

Although the Village wasn't that big—about three square miles—it still took longer than you'd think to canvas it all. Officer James Wilskie was just about to complete his first run, which consisted mainly of driving around for deterrence, but also included getting out of his squad car and walking some areas that couldn't be seen from the road. He was a few hours in to his shift and it had, so far, been a normal, quiet night in Ashbelle, just how he liked it.

The Ashbelle Police Department had seen its share of officers leave to pursue more action in bigger towns and cities but, as far as Wilskie was concerned, this was the perfect job. He was born and raised in Ashbelle and had, after his stint in the army, returned home to join the Ashbelle PD. This was his hometown and he loved being in a position to keep it safe and to give back to the Village that had been so good to him.

Wilskie was just finishing one of his walks along the railroad trestle to check for, and scare off, local kids who liked to drink and smoke cigarettes there. Wilskie didn't really care to get any of the local kids in trouble, but it was the same way when he was growing up. The police had to make sure the kids didn't get too comfortable with their illegal activities. If he ever did catch kids, he'd tell them to just get out of here or, if they were too drunk, he'd drive them home or make sure they had a friend who could drive them home safely. He treated the kids with respect and in return, they treated him with respect. He took pride in the connection he had with Village residents, kids and adults alike.

As he reached his squad car, he couldn't quite shake the weird feeling he was having about his earlier interaction with Earl. He had known Earl forever; Ashbelle was a town where everyone knew everyone. They were a grade apart in school and they had played all manner of sports growing up together. Earl wasn't much of an athlete, but he had heart and always gave his best effort. Wilskie, on the other hand, was an all-conference basketball guard and all-conference tailback in football. He saw Earl occasionally, mainly at church, a cookout, or around town, and knew him as a semi-quiet guy but one who was always nice and willing to lend a hand. He knew Earl was best friends with Victor, who Wilskie had also known since he was a little kid. He considered both of them to be all-around nice guys.

That's why it was eating at him that Earl had seemed so nervous to see him. He also found it very strange that Earl was also apparently not planning on going to the union meeting. Earl always went to those meetings and it was strange that if he wasn't, that he'd be just walking around town. Also, he didn't look sick like he claimed. Wilskie prided himself on not nosing in to other peoples' business—a man had a right to his privacy. That's why he didn't like to pepper people with questions about what they were up to and only asked Earl because he considered them friends.

As Wilskie started up the squad car to do another canvas of the Village, he thought of reasons why Earl had acted so oddly. Was he drunk? Was he upset? Was he confused? He didn't seem like any of those things. Wilskie shifted the car into drive and made a mental note to himself to discreetly ask Earl if everything was all right the next time he saw him.

—◄o►—

After about fifteen minutes of slow moving by flashlight, Lenny, Vic, and Earl had made it to the end of the corridor and were now at the tunnel entrance located inside of the factory. Here, the ground angled upward to reach the factory. Victor realized this could make rolling the bomb down difficult, but figured with three guys, they could probably avoid losing control of the cart the bomb would be on.

At the top of the ramp connecting the tunnel to the factory, the door was open just enough where they could get their hands inside and open the door all the way. Fortunately, the doorway looked plenty wide enough for the bomb to fit through easily.

"I'm surprised this door is so big," said Earl.

"Probably so that if they had to evacuate the factory quickly, they could fit men through four or five at a time instead of one or two, which would really slow the process down," replied Victor. "If you notice, too, the door in to this closet is wider than normal for the same reason."

"I never even noticed. I was in such a rush," replied a surprised Earl.

"If you two ladies are done discussing the damn doors, can we please get on with it?" said Lenny.

It was strange for Earl and Victor to enter the factory floor this way and, even though they knew the place like the back of their hands, it seemed like a different world to them—dark, quiet, and almost creepy. They had agreed that there would be no flashlights in the factory as an outside guard might see the light coming from inside and may come in to investigate. The men could hear quite a bit of noise coming from the union hall, which was great.

"You union boys like to party, don't you?" asked Lenny.

Both Earl and Victor turned on him and shushed him.

"Sorry, wow. You guys are tight, aren't you?" asked Lenny.

"Just keep your voice down, idiot," said Victor.

"Don't call me an idiot or I'll knock your teeth out!" replied Lenny.

"Guys, stop it! Just keep it down," added Earl as he stepped between the two men.

"He's right. Let's put our issues aside for now," said Vic.

"Yeah, for now we will," replied Lenny.

After a few deep breaths, Victor said, "Earl, go grab a cart and Lenny and I will go over by the bombs."

As Vic and Lenny walked towards the northwest corner of the factory toward the bombs, Lenny followed Victor's every step as he didn't want to run in to any equipment. Once they reached the bomb area, Lenny said, "Wow, I never imagined there'd be this many bombs in here. We should sneak out a bunch of them," said Lenny.

"No, only one, and we better hope they don't miss it!" snapped Victor.

"All right, all right, I'm just saying more bombs, more money," replied Lenny, still talking too loudly. "I guess my buddy only has room for one on his trailer anyway."

Earl came back hustling toward them with one of the carts he had grabbed from the other side of the loading dock.

"Good job, Earl. Let's roll it by one of the ones in the middle. Hopefully if we grab one from there and spread the remaining ones out, this row won't look shorter than the others and they won't notice they're missing one," whispered Vic.

Earl and Lenny followed Victor to one of the bombs in the row closest to the tunnel entrance. "Park and lock the cart here, Earl," said Vic, pointing to a specific bomb.

Next, the men surrounded the bomb and got in position to lift it on to the cart.

"Wait, wait, wait, how do we know this thing won't explode?" said a worried Lenny.

"They don't leave the factory live, Lenny," said Victor. "They arm them when they get to wherever it is they're going."

"Yeah, yeah, I, um, I knew that...I was just messing with you guys," replied Lenny with a nervous laugh.

The men lifted the bomb on to the cart. The bombs were heavy, but workers in two-man teams loaded and unloaded them every day. Once the cart was loaded, the men strapped it in to place and began to roll it toward the tunnel entrance when all of a sudden, Lenny squealed in pain, "My toe! Damn it, my toe!"

Earl and Victor looked at each other astounded at how loud Lenny had just screamed, "Shut up, you fool!" hissed Victor.

"Up yours, Victor! I stubbed my toe on something. I can't see where I'm going in here," replied Lenny as he leaned on the cart while holding his foot.

"You are going to get us caught!" said Victor as he shoved a finger in to Lenny's chest.

"Shut up! It's so loud around here, no one heard me. Relax," replied Lenny with an annoying smirk on his face.

"Let's just keep moving and get out of here, please," said Earl.

Just as they were about to roll the cart further, a door from the other end of factory floor flung open and the men saw a guard walk in and begin scanning the factory floor with a blindingly bright flashlight.

"Everyone get down!" said Vic.

All three men hit the floor.

"Don't make a sound," whispered Vic as the guard got closer. They couldn't see him, but they could see the light and hear the guard's steps, which echoed loudly in the vast, empty, quiet space.

"He's getting closer. What are we going to do if he sees us?" whispered Earl.

"Let's hope for his sake he doesn't see us," said Lenny.

"Both of you just shut up and keep quiet," whispered Victor.

After what seemed like an eternity, the men heard the flashlight click off and the door shut.

"That was close. You almost got us caught, dumbass!" snapped Victor.

"Sorry guys, really," said Lenny in a surprisingly apologetic voice. "Good thing your guards are too lazy to actually walk the whole factory floor."

The men hopped up with a little extra adrenaline and rolled the bomb in to the tunnel entrance, quickly shutting the door in the janitor's closet behind them and replacing the cleaning supplies so it looked like no one had been in there. All three knew they weren't done yet, but a palpable relief had set in. They had actually accomplished the seemingly impossible and dangerous task of stealing a United States Air Force bomb.

"We did it, boys!" said Lenny.

"Not so fast .We still need to get this thing out of here and on that trailer," replied Victor.

"Hard part's over, that's all I'm saying," said Lenny.

Chapter Sixteen
1944

James Wilskie was on the back half of his shift as he put his cruiser in park near the front of the school. Part of his nightly routine was to walk around the school to make sure no local kids had decided to vandalize the place, break in, or climb up to the top of the school to have a good time with some beers. Wilskie came down hard on any vandalizing or breaking in; this was his school in his town and he wouldn't take it easy on kids who were damaging the place. Fortunately, it rarely happened, but when it did, he and the other officers made examples of those responsible. The rooftop partying was a bit of a different story. Kids had been doing it for years, himself included. Generally speaking, it was harmless—no damage done, relatively safe as there were plenty of easy ways to get up and down, and just kids being kids.

He smiled to himself as he thought back to some of the times he and his friends had had on top of the school; they were great memories, but brought to mind great sadness also as two of his very good friends from high school had recently been killed in the war, one in Europe and the other in the Pacific theatre. He said a quick prayer of thanks that he had made it home safe and sound before continuing his patrol.

He walked the front of the school with his flashlight in his hand, but not on so as not to give himself away. If there were punks causing damage, he wanted to catch them red-handed. If there was rooftop partying going on, he enjoyed sneaking up on the kids and scaring them half to death before playfully telling them to get off the school and go home. It was kind of an unwritten rule that officers didn't come down on these kids. It actually led to a sort of respect between the police and the local high schoolers; the police let the kids know they could do something about it and chose not to, and the kids knew that the officers weren't a bunch of hard asses looking to ruin their fun.

As he rounded the front of the school, he was happy to see no damage being done, but actually a little sad to see no partying going on. It was a fun part of growing up in Ashbelle and he hoped to see the tradition live on.

Wilskie had continued around the side and almost the entire rear of the school without incident and was about to head back to his cruiser when he heard a real faint sound. It didn't sound like voices, but almost like a knocking sound. He turned on his flashlight and pointed it at the doors on the back side of the school, but saw nothing out of the ordinary. Next, he approached the different doors and looked in them through the glass and double-checked to make sure they were locked, but didn't see any sign of anything odd. *Maybe my old ass is just hearing things,* he thought to himself with a smile.

Convinced that it was all in his head, he turned the back corner of school and began again toward his squad car, but then he heard it again.

"What the hell is that?" Wilskie said out loud to himself as he strained his head to try to zero in on where the noise was coming from. He was convinced it wasn't coming from the school, having just walked the entire perimeter, so he started to head away from the building toward the tennis courts.

At this point, he had determined that whatever the noise was, it must be coming from the tennis court area; he figured it was either a broken piece of equipment hitting a post or a can or bottle blowing in to the fence. As he got closer, he raised his flashlight so he could see the tennis courts, which were down the hill. He was never a competitive tennis player, but he shook his head and laughed to himself as he remembered the time in gym class when he had been playing and had embarrassingly hit himself in the mouth with his racquet as he was at the net and a ball was coming at his face. He had busted open his lip and had had to leave school to go get stitches. *Dumbass,* he thought to himself.

Snapping out of it, he scanned the tennis courts with his light but didn't see anything that could be responsible for the noise. Then he heard it again, and this time it was louder than before. Knowing he had to investigate further, Wilskie made his way down the hill until he was level with the tennis courts. He was glad it wasn't wet, as that hill had led to many slips and falls when it was. Still seeing nothing on the courts, he threw the light up on to the hillside, but still saw nothing. He shook his head, but then heard the sound again and quickly turned his light in the direction he was now sure it was coming from. He climbed about halfway up the hill and what he saw next both confused and startled him: There was a metal door that seemed to be built in to the hill that he had never seen before, and the door had a pile of dirt next to it. After shining his light upon the door, he quickly realized what the cause of the noise was: a strange-looking contraption connected to the door that was banging against it in the slight wind. Although at first it looked like a stethoscope, Wilskie realized after looking closer that the end connected to the doorway looked like a plunger, not like the typical ending of a stethoscope. *What the hell is going on here?* he thought to himself.

At this point, Wilskie turned his flashlight to a very thin beam and drew his gun. This was the first time that he had ever had to draw his gun while on duty. He had hoped he would never have had to; he'd been in enough gunfights in the war to last a lifetime.

Next, Wilskie slowly reached out and attempted to pull the door open; he was surprised to see that it was slightly ajar. He proceeded to carefully and quietly open it just enough to stick his head in to see if he could see or hear anyone. He tried to shake the feeling of how strange this whole door-in-the-hillside thing was and re-focus on finding out what the hell was going on. Again, he stuck his head in the doorway, but still couldn't see or hear anything. He knew he was going to have to go inside and see what this doorway led to and who was in there.

As he entered, he noticed how extremely dark it was inside. The only light at all was a small amount coming in from a streetlight near the tennis courts. Before he proceeded, he had to make his flashlight beam brighter and did so begrudgingly, not wanting to give his presence away, so he lifted it only as high as he needed to see in front of him. As he moved forward, he realized that this was some kind of tunnel; it looked very new, as there were no cobwebs, bugs, or dead animals on the floor, ceilings, or walls. This tunnel, like the door, was clearly professionally done and had probably cost a fortune to install. "But where did it go to and how could something like this possibly have been kept a secret?" wondered Wilskie.

With his gun still drawn, he kept going down the tunnel, stopping every few feet to listen for anything that might tell if there were people inside. Not hearing anything, he made his way further in to the tunnel until he froze in place as he heard someone yelling, "My toe, damn it! My toe!"

Wilskie cut off his flashlight and put his back to the wall. At this point, Wilskie could tell that the noise was still from quite a ways in front of him, so he quickly moved forward while keeping in contact with the wall to avoid having to turn on his flashlight. After a minute, he saw light coming down from an area of tunnel that ramped up quite a bit; he assumed that this is where the tunnel ended, but he still wasn't sure where he was in the Village.

As Wilskie remained pinned against the wall with his gun in one hand and flashlight in the other, he told himself to remain calm and control his breathing; that advice had saved him more than once during the war. He could now hear several jovial voices coming down the ramp toward him. It sounded like the group of men—he couldn't tell how many there were— was rolling something heavy.

Knowing that the group would soon be within sight, Wilskie's grip on his gun tightened and he prepared himself to confront them. He sincerely hoped that it was just some local kids who had somehow stumbled on to this tunnel and were just investigating where it went. That hope was soon vanquished when he saw three men and his jaw dropped as he instantly recognized Earl and Victor.

Wilskie knew that with their flashlight on and back on level ground, they were going to see him soon, so when they were about twenty-five feet away, he flicked on his light, stepped out in to the middle of the tunnel, and forcefully said, "Ashbelle Police, stop right there and put your hands up!"

After securing the cart, Earl and Victor immediately stepped away from the bomb and raised their hands as instructed. Not surprisingly, Lenny didn't do as he was told; rather, he put his hands on his hips and glared at Wilskie.

"What in the hell is going on here?" yelled Wilskie.

Earl and Victor looked at each other, and Earl said, "Jimmy, hey, what are you doing, man? Put the gun down. We're all friends here."

"Can't," replied Wilskie, "at least not until you tell me what the hell is going on here!"

Victor took a step forward, causing Wilskie to take aim at his chest, and said, "Well, Jimmy, I'm not going to lie to you and say that this isn't what it looks like. What we have here is a bomb that we are taking off of the company's hands. And what you're standing in is one of several secret tunnels built by the federal government for workers to escape quickly if the company were attacked for being a munitions factory."

Wilskie was trying his best to wrap his head around what he had just heard while at the same time control the situation. "You can't just steal a bomb from the company, Victor. I have to take you guys in for this. Now get down on the ground and put your hands behind your back."

"We could do that, Jimmy," said Victor, "or we could handle this another way."

Wilskie replied, "What the hell are you talking about, Victor? There is no other way to handle this!"

"That's where you're wrong, Jimmy," continued Victor. "As I said, this tunnel gives us access to a factory that is chalk full of bombs like these that fetch a killing on the black market. We could all pretend this never happened, and we'll cut you in on this and whatever future bombs we sell. What do you say?"

Wilskie shook his head, saying, "No way, man. I don't want anything to do with this. Now get on the ground and put your hands behind your head. Don't make me ask again."

Earl was already on the ground, hands behind his head, and said, "Guys, get down like he said!"

"All right, Jimmy, we're getting on the ground, just like you asked," said Victor as he and, surprisingly, Lenny began to do as they were told.

Wilskie lowered his gun, put his flashlight on the ground, and removed several sets of handcuffs from his belt. As he approached the trio lying in a row, he said, "I can't believe you guys would throw it all away over shit like this."

Wilskie began to slowly approach Lenny. He wanted to get him cuffed first, as he had no idea who he was, and he could tell from his refusal to put his hands up that he was likely to cause trouble. Wilskie was standing above Lenny's back ready to place the cuffs on, gun pointed down, when like a bolt of lightning Lenny rolled over, pointed a gun straight at Wilskie's head, and shot. The sound was deafening and rang out through the tunnel as Jimmy Wilskie fell to the ground, dead with a bullet wound square in the middle of his forehead.

Earl yelled, "No! Lenny, what have you done?"

Victor screamed out, "Holy shit, Lenny! What the hell did you do that for?"

Neither Earl nor Victor had any clue that besides shovels and flashlights, Lenny had packed a little something extra.

As he stood up, Lenny looked directly at Earl and said in a surprisingly calm manner, "I had to, brother. He was going to arrest us. I couldn't let that happen. I am not going back to prison."

For what seemed like an eternity, Earl and Victor just sat frozen, looking at Wilskie's dead body as blood flowed from his forehead.

After a minute, Lenny shook both guys out of their shocked state, saying, "Guys, get your asses up and let's get this bomb out of here."

"We-we-we can't do that…" stammered Earl.

"Yeah, what are we going to do with the body?" asked Victor.

"Nothing at all," replied a stone-cold Lenny.

"What do you mean nothing? We can't just leave him lying here," said Earl.

"Yes, we can, and that's exactly what we are going to do," replied Lenny. "And here's why: This factory is never going to get bombed. Even if the Krauts were able to get to America to do that, they'd never make it to the Midwest. So, we are going to leave him here, roll this bomb out, and seal this tunnel up like it was before. And, listen to me extremely carefully on this, we will never ever speak of this to anyone—ever. This man, who was in the wrong place at the wrong time—and I'm sorry I had to shoot him—is in his burial tomb. If he is ever found, it's going to be once we are all long gone. Do you two understand me?"

Earl and Victor looked at each other, both surprised by Lenny's calmness and directness, and nodded their heads.

"Good, let's go, then," said Lenny.

The three men grabbed the cart and began toward the tunnel exit. As they rolled by Wilskie's body, Earl whispered to Victor, "This isn't right. This isn't right."

Victor whispered back, "I know, but what choice do we have?"

As the men approached the tunnel exit, Lenny ordered Victor and Earl to stay with the bomb while he went to get his friend who was waiting nearby with the trailer and make sure no one else was around.

It seemed to take forever waiting for Lenny to get back; while they waited for him, Earl slid down the wall, sat down, and began to cry.

Victor sat down next to Earl and put his arm around him. "It's okay. Everything's going to be okay. Lenny's an asshole, but he's right. We're going to be fine."

Earl lifted his head up, looked Victor straight in the eyes, and said, "Fine? Fine? I'm never going to be fine. If I just would've told Lenny I wasn't interested in this stupid plot of his and helped him do it, Jimmy Wilskie would still be alive instead of rotting in this damn tunnel! His death is my fault. I can't believe this happened."

As Victor was about to reply, they heard the door open back up and Lenny waved them forward, saying, "Get your asses up and stop crying like a little baby, Earl! If you had pulled the door all the way shut like I told you to, none of this would've happened!" What Lenny failed to mention was that it was his mistake for leaving his modified stethoscope on the door, but he had removed it and didn't see a need to tell them about it.

"Hey man, back off!" said Victor as he stood up and pointed at Lenny. "Some serious shit happened here tonight and he's taking it pretty hard. Can't you just leave him alone?"

"Shut up, Vic. He needs to act like a man and pull himself together," replied Lenny.

"You're an asshole, Lenny," said Victor as he helped Earl up off the ground.

Lenny looked Victor straight in the eye, took a step toward him, and said, "If you don't shut the hell up, you'll be the next one with a bullet in the head. Now listen, he's here with the trailer and the coast is clear. We've got to go, now!"

Lenny opened the door all the way and then the three men rolled the bomb out of the tunnel and began to head toward the waiting truck that was idling on the road beside the tennis courts. It wasn't easy getting the bomb to the truck considering the slope of the hill, but they managed to do it successfully and rather quickly.

Once they reached the trailer, a dangerous-looking man hopped out of the driver's side door and said to roll the cart up on to the trailer. A minute later, the bomb and cart were loaded on the flat bed trailer and Lenny and his seedy-looking friend threw a tarp over it and tied it down. Lenny said a few things to his friend that Vic and Earl couldn't hear, and then the man jumped back in to the truck and took off. They had done it; the bomb was stolen, loaded up, and on its way to be delivered.

After the truck was out of sight, Lenny said, "Nice job, boys. Now all we have to do is go replace the dirt and cover that door up, and we can go on with our lives. Let's go."

Earl and Victor followed Lenny back to the tunnel exit and they spent the next hour in complete silence putting the dirt back over the door so that you could never tell it was even disturbed. After they had covered up about half the door, Victor realized that his service pin he always wore on his jacket was missing. He said he needed to go back and get it to which Lenny replied, "Try to go get it and I'll kill you…we need to get this covered up and get the hell out of here, you got me?!" Victor wanted to kill Lenny, but begrudgingly gave in.

After they were done, Lenny looked both Earl and Victor in the eyes and said, "Listen, you guys are going to have to find that cop's squad car and get rid it. I don't care how. Just get rid of it. I'll be in touch when I have the money. And, one last thing, remember what I said in there…or else."

As Lenny took off running in the direction of the cemetery, Earl and Victor stood there trying to make sense of how what should've been just stealing a bomb had turned in to a cold-blooded murder.

Earl looked at Victor and said, "I can't take this, man. I'm going to the cops and admitting the whole thing."

Victor grabbed Earl by the shoulders and spoke to him like a father to a child, "Okay, okay, but think about this first. If you talk, we're going to spend the rest of our lives in prison and that's if we don't get executed! What we did here was a federal crime—treason. Not to mention participating in a cold-blooded murder. Your conscience may be clear if you go to the cops, but is that worth it? Think about your wife, your kids, your job," said Vic. "How are they going to feel? How are they going to be raised without their daddy and Uncle Vic around? Jimmy's dead and that's horrible, but what good does it do to say anything about it now? This whole thing is almost done and then life can get back to normal. Also, Lenny's right. No one is going to be in this tunnel until we are dead and gone, if ever, so you do what you have to do, but you think about all that first."

Vic began to walk away toward the front of the school.

"Where are you going?" asked Earl.

"To find Wilskie's squad car. You coming with me or are you going to confess?"

Earl looked at the ground and then said, "I'm coming with you, Vic. Let's finish this thing."

On their way to the front of the school, Earl said, "You know what else. If I had shut the door all the way, Wilskie would never have known we were in there."

"Don't buy that for one second, Earl. I bet your brother left that damn stethoscope thingy on the door or something. Wilskie would never have seen the door open from up here. He must've heard something and it was probably that thing hitting the door."

"You really think?" asked Earl, trying to hold back tears.

"Yes, I do, and your brother is a big enough asshole to make you think it was your fault," replied Victor. "Now, let's get up to the front of the school and find the squad car."

Earl decided then and there that his brother was a terrible person who clearly didn't love him.

As the men reached the front of the school, they saw Wilskie's squad car parked on the street right in front of the school.

"There it is," said Earl, pointing at the squad car.

"Yeah, unfortunately right under that streetlight," replied Vic. "We're going to have to move fast and quietly to avoid waking up someone in one of these houses."

"If you can get us in the car, I can hot wire it," said Earl.

"Really? I didn't know you knew how to do that," said Vic with a surprised look on his face.

"Yeah, Lenny taught me when we were younger," said Earl.

"I'm not surprised," replied Vic.

As they approached the vehicle, Victor grabbed a small, jagged rock from the side of the road. He walked up to the driver's side window, looked around, and threw it at close range in to the window. Fortunately, the window just spider-webbed around the hole caused by the rock, so it didn't smash and make a loud noise. Vic pulled out a few pieces of glass, laid them on the ground, and reached in and unlocked the door. Earl ran to the passenger's side and hopped in after Vic unlocked his door.

"All right, let's see here," said Earl as he worked quickly, pulling wires out from under the dash. After about a minute, the car roared to life.

"Where do you think we should dump it?" asked Victor.

"Not sure, but we need to make sure no one sees us driving around in it," replied Earl.

A minute later as they were debating where to dump the car, both men jumped as the radio chirped, "Jimmy, Jimmy, come in. Jimmy, Jimmy, you there?"

"You going to answer it?" asked Earl nervously.

"No way! They'll know I'm not Wilskie. I can't fake that," replied Vic.

After another attempt to reach Wilskie, the radio fell silent.

"We need to figure out where in the hell we're taking this thing and fast. With Wilskie not responding, they're going to send someone else out to look for his squad car. We've got to get this thing off the streets," said Vic.

"Should we just drive it out in to the country and leave it?" said Earl.

"No way. Someone will find it soon, plus we might get pulled over driving it by some curious sheriff's deputy wondering what an Ashbelle Police Department car is doing outside the Village limits," replied Victor.

"Good point. I've got an idea," said Earl.

"Let's hear it because I'm drawing a blank and we've got to get moving," replied Victor.

"There's that Village maintenance building on the south side of town, down the road past that area you're always saying should be a golf course some day," said Earl. "Remember a year or so ago when my brother-in-law who works for the Public Works Department took us there to show us that fishing hole near it?"

"Yeah, I remember. Keep going," replied Victor anxiously.

"Anyway, that day, while I was walking behind the main building to take a leak, I noticed that there were a dozen or so rusted and unused Village vehicles just sitting there behind the building near the back wall. I'm sure that no one ever looks back there. If we could ditch the vehicle in there, no one would ever find it…at least not until you and I are dead and gone," said Earl.

"Don't you think they ever go back there looking for parts or something?" asked Victor.

"I don't think so. None of the cars looked picked apart or anything," replied Earl.

"Okay, fine. I can't think of anything else. Let's do it," replied Victor.

Earl said, "Take a weird route there, though. Less chance of being seen than on one of the main roads."

Victor nodded as he pulled away from the curb and headed toward the maintenance building using side streets whenever possible. Fortunately, no one seemed to be out and they were able to get there without, hopefully, being seen.

Victor cut the lights and pulled the car behind the building. They sat in the car for a second making sure that no employee was working late, but the place was dark and the only vehicles they could see were Village ones, no personal employee vehicles.

"Are we just going to leave it here?" asked Earl nervously.

"I think what we should do first before ditching it back here is to try to get the lights off and beat it up a little bit so it blends in with the other pieces of crap out here," replied Victor.

The men got out of the car and were staring at the vehicle when Earl said, "That's going to be hard because this thing is like two years old and looks brand new."

"Yeah, but we've got to try," said Victor. "Let's pop the trunk and see what tools are back there that we can use to trash this thing."

The men opened the trunk and fished out a tool set and a couple of batons and went to work removing the lights from the top of the car and then slid them beneath the vehicle. Next they took the batons and whacked the vehicle about a dozen times each so that it started to resemble its new neighbors. Stepping back, they took in their handiwork.

Earl said, "That was fun."

"It was, buddy, but it's still too clean. We need to rub some mud on it or something," replied Vic.

The men went in to the nearby woods and dug up some dirt and rubbed it on the vehicle. "That's better," said Victor. "Looks like she's been here a while. Just one more thing to do. Hand me that knife from the tool set."

Earl handed it to him, not sure what he was planning on doing. He found out shortly as Vic walked around the vehicles and slashed all four tires. "There. Hopefully that'll make it seem even more like it's been here a while."

"Let's get out of here and pretend this night never happened," replied Earl.

"Sounds good, buddy. Sounds good," replied Victor.

Chapter Seventeen
1997

As Preston left the courthouse, he called Sharon and asked her to call in all available Ashbelle PD officers and also call the sheriff's department to request help in executing the search warrant that he had in his hand. "Tell them to be ready to go at the police department in two hours."

Two hours later, Preston was loaded up and ready to go in the Ashbelle PD parking lot with three Ashbelle PD officers and, thankfully, three sheriff's deputies. He thanked them all for coming and gave them a quick rundown of the situation. "As you all have heard by now, we've got a boy missing in the Village and I have a very strong suspicion that he is at the house of this man," said Preston as he held up a picture of Victor.

"There is a very good chance that his grandson, who's a real pain-in-the-ass tough guy, by the way—will be there when we arrive or will show up during our search. Be aware of this guy. He's a loose cannon who is also a violent drunk," said Preston as he held up a picture of Sam. "If there aren't any questions, let's get to it."

A quick five minutes later, two Ashbelle PD and two sheriff's department cruisers pulled up in front of Victor's house. Victor, who was sitting in his recliner, saw the cruisers pull up and Preston and the other officers pop immediately out of their vehicles.

"Damn son of a bitch!" said Victor to himself. He wanted to leave, but he realized that wasn't happening, and he also realized that this time not answering or refusing to let Preston in was not going to be an option. Although upset and worried that Preston might find what he was looking for, Vic was glad he had asked Sam to come over and remove the kitchen carpeting and get rid of the dirt pile in the garage.

Preston banged on the front door, fully expecting to have to force his way in when it was suddenly opened by a surprisingly friendly Victor.

"Hello Preston, is that your stupid warrant in your hand?" asked Victor with a cocky smile on his face.

"Sure is, Victor, and I'm going to tear your house apart this time unless you tell me where the murder weapon is and where Chris's body is," replied Preston, unable to withhold his contempt for Victor.

"No need to be so hostile. Be my guest. I've got nothing to hide. I told you before that I had nothing to do with that kid disappearing," replied a still-smirking Victor as he plopped down in to his recliner.

Preston sent a few of his men around to the back and then entered the home with the others. "You two, go check the basement to see if I missed anything down there." Meanwhile, Preston went straight for the kitchen, knowing what he was going to find. Sure enough, the kitchen had its carpet ripped out. "Hey Vic, getting some new carpet in the kitchen?" he asked as he stared at the bare concrete floor.

"Oh yeah, figured it's about time. Got tired of looking at that stain on the carpet," Vic replied.

Preston clenched his fists and left out the back door, heading straight for the garage. When he was about ten feet away, a car flew up the driveway and slammed on its brakes, almost hitting two officers standing in front of the garage door.

Sam opened the car door, slammed it, and walked straight at Preston. "I told you to leave my grandpa alone. Now get the hell off his property before I sue you for harassment!"

"Relax, big fella, this warrant says I can be here and search whatever I want. What it doesn't say is that I know where Chris's body is. It also does-n't say that once I find the body, I'm going to arrest you for murder because I know that your granddad, no matter how much of a tough ass he thinks he is, couldn't have killed Chris, so that leaves you. Why don't you just save us all some time and tell me how you did it?"

Sam took a step back and then, with a cocky smile on his face, said, "I think you're bluffing." Sam was attempting to look confident, but Preston could tell he was actually betraying his fear underneath.

"Really? Well, stick around and watch the show, and then you'll see that I'm not bluffing," replied Preston as he continued toward the garage.

After a few steps, Preston felt a pain in his right arm as Sam reached out, grabbed it, and squeezed it, stopping Preston in his tracks. Sam leaned in and whispered, "If you go in that garage, I'll kill you."

Preston put up his hand to stop the officers who were coming to his aid. "It's okay, boys, I've got this." Preston calmly looked down at the arm Sam was holding and said, "Ever been tased before? No? Well, if you don't release me immediately, you will be. I've tased guys far bigger than you and believe me, you don't want that."

Sam glared at Preston before reluctantly letting go of his arm and stormed inside to talk to Victor.

Preston called over the two officers and said, "One of you stick to the grandson like glue, and one of you pull your squad car up behind his ve-hicle; I don't want either of them to think they can run off."

Preston tried to enter the garage. It was harder than he thought it would be, as there had been a new lock put on the door, one much stronger than he anticipated. He thought he was going to have to wait for someone to bring him a lock cutter out of one of the squad cars, but then he decided to just break the glass in the door instead. "Oops, my mistake," he said out loud, bringing a chuckle from the officer who had pulled up behind Sam's car.

Next, Preston reached in through the broken glass and unlocked the deadbolt from the inside. Once inside the garage, he turned on the light. Even with it on, the garage was still dark, so Preston turned on his flashlight. Based on what Andrew had told him, he knew what to expect, so he sidestepped the piles of junk strewn all around the garage and headed toward the back. As expected, the back happened to be the one open space in the garage. He noticed the dirt pile that Andrew described was missing, but he knew that it would be based on what the officer who saw Sam drive away from the house earlier had told him.

Preston took a second look down at the ground; the old concrete had been removed and there was dirt in a large rectangular shape that had clearly been put there recently. Preston clinched his fists again and was surprised to feel a tear rolling down his cheek. He wiped it away and took a few deep breaths, still hoping that he wasn't looking at what he knew he was looking at.

He dreaded doing what needed to be done, but knew he had to dig in search of Chris's body.

Preston walked back out of the garage in to the fresh air and called over the officers that weren't keeping an eye on Victor and Sam and told them to go to the police station and grab several portable lights and some shovels. The officers all looked down, as they knew at that instant that Preston had found what they were all hoping he wasn't going to. In a minute they were gone and Preston walked back in to the garage to wait.

About twenty minutes later, the officers were back with the lights and shovels. Preston and another officer started digging; the others had gone back in to the house to look for the murder weapon. Unfortunately, it didn't take long before the officer across from Preston took a step back and said, "Holy shit."

"What is it?" asked Preston.

The officer didn't say a word, but just pointed. Preston walked over to him for a better view and saw what appeared to be a tennis shoe. Preston knew then and there that they had found Chris.

Preston stood there for a second, head lowered, trying to fight back tears. In his head, he was thinking to himself, *What a waste. This young kid killed because he found that stupid tunnel and dared to ask an old man about it.* Preston wanted to walk in the house and beat the old man and his grandson to death; that seemed like the only true justice for this heinous and truly unnecessary murder. He knew that even once found guilty, both men would get life in prison, as Wisconsin didn't have the death penalty and that seemed grossly unfair to him. After a minute, Preston looked at the officer with him in the garage and ordered him to go inside and arrest both Victor and Sam and put them in a squad car.

Preston decided at this point to stop digging and call the coroner and the sheriff's department; the Ashbelle PD didn't have a forensics team and he didn't want to contaminate the crime scene and give either Sam or Vic a loophole to get out of this thing.

An hour or so later, the coroner and forensics team arrived and most of the officers left except for the Ashbelle PD officers, who Preston needed for crowd control, as a large group had gathered at the end of the driveway and on the sidewalk. News traveled fast in a town this size and people were already asking what was going on and if it had anything to do with the search for Chris. Fortunately, the work being done was in the garage, so Preston didn't have to worry about privacy. Preston spent the next hour watching the coroner and forensics team slowly excavate the area. When they began to reach Chris's body, Preston almost lost it. It took everything he had to not cry, yell, or punch a wall or break something. He decided he needed to get out of the garage and stepped outside for some fresh air. He knew he was on display out here and took several deep breaths to calm himself.

After a minute, he looked toward the gathered crowd and saw at the front Chris's mom and stepdad. Chris's mom was crying as Chris' stepdad was holding her. He wanted to go over to them and tell them it was going to be all right, but it wasn't; he had just found their son's dead body and he knew he'd have to tell them about it soon. Preston looked up at the sky, trying to hold back the tears. He was about to go and talk to Chris's mom when one of the forensics team members came up to him and said, "Chief, you've got to come and see this."

Preston sighed and said, "Okay, right behind you," as he headed back in to the garage.

Preston had no idea what he was about to see, but the first thing he noticed was that Chris's body had been pulled out of the hole and was lying on a tarp next to it. Trying his best to not get emotional again, he looked away from the body toward the hole.

He saw two men in the hole, and the one who appeared to be in charge said, "You aren't going to believe this, but there's another body in here."

"What?" replied a shocked Preston. "What are you talking about?"

"Well, I shouldn't really say 'another body.' This is a skeleton who appears to be dressed in a uniform of some kind."

Unable to comprehend or fathom what he was being told, he got down in to the hole with the men and saw what they were looking at; he could hardly believe his eyes. Was Victor a serial killer? Who was this man? He got down on his hands and knees and dusted off the chest some more where he saw two patches on the skeleton's chest: *Ashbelle Police Department* and *Wilskie*.

He stood up and began processing in his mind that the body of the one missing police officer in Ashbelle's history had been found. After wrapping his mind around that, he tried to make sense of why Wilskie's body was under Chris's in Victor's garage. Then it hit him: The boys had been honest and not mistaken about what they had seen in the tunnel, and he felt a rush of guilt for not believing them.

But how did the body end up here? Why had it been moved here? And by whom?

After telling everyone in the garage to keep the finding of Wilskie a secret for now, he left the garage and headed towards Chris's mom and stepdad.

—◄o►—

Preston arrived back at his office after the longest, saddest day of his life. In addition to finding Chris's murdered body, he had had to tell Chris's parents, the press, and the Village residents that one of their bright young children had been murdered. On top of all of that, he had found Wilskie, the man whose sudden disappearance while on duty had been the source of rumors and stories in the Village for over fifty years. Preston never drank on the job, but tonight he made an exception and pulled out a small bottle of bourbon he kept in his desk drawer. "Sharon!" he yelled.

"Yes, Chief," she replied from the doorway.

"Have a seat. I need a drinking buddy right now," he said as Sharon smiled and sat down in front of the desk.

After they had each taken a few pulls off the bottle, Sharon said, "I'd be all up for finishing this thing with you, but Sam and Vic are downstairs. We're holding them before bringing them to the county jail so you can talk to them."

"Okay, I better head down there, then. Thanks Sharon, I needed that after today," he said as he raised himself out of his chair.

"Anytime," said Sharon as she began to leave his office. She stopped at the doorway, turned around, and added, "People are talking, of course. They're wondering how Chris's body ended up in Victor's garage and what connection the two had. People are also saying that a second body was found in the garage. Is that true?"

"A rumor, Sharon. Just a rumor."

"Sure, Chief," said Sharon with a wink as she stood up and left the office.

Preston had ordered Sam and Vic separated, so he decided to talk to Sam first. After grabbing himself a quick cup of coffee, he headed downstairs to the interrogation room where Sam was.

Preston entered the room, fully expecting Sam to be cocky and completely uncooperative, so he had ordered Sam to be handcuffed to the table. Preston was shocked when he entered the room and saw a defeated-looking Sam with tears running down his face.

Preston calmly sat down and looked at Sam. "Son, I know we've had our differences, but play time is over. We know you killed Chris, or at least were an accessory to the murder. Why don't you save us a lot of time and tell me how it all happened?"

About a half hour later, Preston left the room where he had been interrogating Sam; he was surprised at how quickly Sam had told him everything that happened. This big, tough guy had been brought to tears as he let it all out and kept saying that he did what he did to protect his grandpa. Preston summoned an officer over and told him to head to Victor's house to grab the baseball bat and have it tested for Chris's blood and logged in as evidence. He then proceeded to the room where they had put Victor.

Preston entered the room and looked at Victor. He had not ordered Vic handcuffed, as he wasn't a threat; he looked like a sad old man who had wasted what should have been his golden years. Preston sat down on the chair at the opposite side of the table, looked Victor right in the eye, and said, "How the hell did we get here?"

"What do you mean, Chief?" replied Victor.

Preston was surprised at how at peace Victor seemed, almost like he had finally been able to breathe after fifty years.

"Sam told me everything: how Chris had shown up at your house, how you three had talked, how he had angered you with his questions, how Sam had chased him through the house, and how you killed him in the kitchen with the baseball bat. He also told me about your ordering him to bury Chris in your garage. So, there's no use denying any of it. Sam will be going away for a long, long time, and all he kept saying was that he did it all to protect you. My question for you is how does this all tie to you? Why would you kill a teenager? And what in the world was Wilskie doing buried in your garage?"

Victor leaned back in his chair, took a deep breath, and then began his confession. "It all started back in 1944 before you were even a thought in your daddy's mind..."

After listening to Victor calmly recount the entire story that spanned a half-century, Preston could hardly believe it. It seemed straight out of a movie: a small-town with a big secret (the tunnel), a murder to cover up a secret (the stealing of the bomb), kids discovering the secret many decades later, an old man willing to do whatever it took and willing to destroy several lives to keep that secret. It was almost unbelievable.

"I feel like I should almost thank you, Chief Preston," said Victor.

"Thank me? Why's that?" replied a surprised Preston.

"I held on to all of this for over fifty years. My entire adult life has been built around that damn tunnel and what had happened in it. I've been watching that tunnel entrance for fifty years; lived by that tunnel entrance for fifty years; kept the secret of that tunnel for fifty years; knew Wilskie's body was in there for fifty years; and had to live with the guilt of our crime for fifty years. I sincerely wish I had never ever been made aware of that stupid tunnel and most regrettably of all, now my selfishness has brought my grandson down with me. Listen, I'll be fine—dead in a few years. It doesn't matter what you do with me, but I'll go to my grave knowing the horrible things I had my grandson do, knowing that he did them all for me."

"So Wilskie was a hero, huh?"

"Yes, he should've been given a promotion and medal from the federal government and instead all he got for his good police work was a bullet to the head. Poor bastard," said Vic with a smirk on his face.

"Not to mention his good name and that of his family being slandered in the Village for generations," replied Preston.

"Yeah, well, shit happens," replied a bored-looking Victor.

"Well Vic, I think it's sad that you won't really get punished for this. Like you said, you'll die a peaceful death, albeit in prison soon, but if it were up to me, I'd strap you in to the electric chair and pull the lever myself."

"Whatever, Preston. Just do whatever you need to do," replied a resigned Victor.

Preston stood up and made his way to the door. As he was about to leave, he looked back and said, "One more thing, Vic. I hope you rot in hell."

Chapter Eighteen
1997

As Preston leaned back in his office chair, he got a knock on his door. "Excuse me, sir, but there's an Agent Williams from the FBI here to speak with you," said Sharon.

"Thank you, you can send him back," replied an exhausted Preston.

"Good to finally meet you in person," said Preston as he stood up and shook the FBI agent's hand while making sure to shut the door, much to Sharon's dismay.

Williams replied, "You as well."

"Have a seat," said Preston as he pointed to the couch.

As Williams sat, he said, "How have things been since you all found the bodies of Officer Wilskie and Chris?"

"Well, it's been what? A month now, and I don't think people still think it's real. We're all trying to get back to normal, but this will be with this town forever, you know?"

"I know it doesn't seem like it, but I've seen this type of thing before and you'll be amazed what tragedy can do for a tight-knit community."

"Thanks for saying that. I hope some positive comes from this whole thing."

"We really wanted to say that we at the Bureau want to thank you for keeping the tunnel system's existence and location a secret all this time."

"Well, you should thank those boys who found it. When I was a teenager, I could never have kept something like that a secret," replied Preston.

"What makes you so sure they didn't tell anyone?" asked Williams.

"In a village like Ashbelle, things get around pretty quickly. I would've heard about a story like that if it were floating around."

"Well, they should be thanked. Please pass that on to them for me."

"Will do," replied Preston.

"There's a couple of reasons I'm here today in person rather than telling you all this over the phone. First off, it is time to let this village know about the finding of Officer Wilskie and to tell his story and clear his name. You and I have a press conference scheduled for tomorrow morning. Is that okay with you?"

"More than okay. I've been looking forward to doing that since we found him," replied Preston.

"Good. Secondly, I'm here to tell you that the Bureau would like to keep that tunnel a secret forever for national security purposes; to encourage you to do that, we'd like to do a few things."

"Sure, understandable. What kind of things?"

"First, we'd like to give each of the three boys who, along with Chris, found the tunnel a scholarship of sorts as a thanks for keeping their mouths shut and also as an encouragement to keep them shut in the future. We will say it's a scholarship from the Ashbelle Police Department, not from us. You can just say they were exemplary young citizens or something so people don't ask what it's for. This scholarship will be paid out by you. Is that okay?"

"Sure, I'll name it after Chris."

"I think that's a great idea," replied Williams. "Next, we'd like to provide your department with a donation as a thank-you for all of your help and discretion with this whole situation."

"Wow, thank you. Anything else?" asked Preston.

"Lastly, as the tunnel is still a topic not to be discussed, we need to come up with a story about where, how, and so forth, Wilskie was finally found that won't arouse suspicion. I'd love, as much as you, to tell everyone that that asshole Victor was involved and sully his name further, but the truth raises too many questions, so we need an alternate story. Any ideas?" asked Williams

"I've actually been thinking about that as well, and I think I have a story that will work."

"Let's hear it," said Williams.

"Along with Wilskie disappearing all those years ago, his squad car also disappeared. That helped lead to nasty rumors that he had just driven off duty to who knows where—a real shame what rumors have been associated with him in this village. Anyways, Victor told me where to find the squad car and how he and his friend ditched it the night of Wilskie's murder. Crazy thing is, it's been under our noses all this time."

"What do you mean?" asked a puzzled Williams.

"We, like most towns, have a village garage with a yard full of old junk that gets kept for way too long and is never, ever gone through. Some of those items are vehicles that are kept in case of spare parts."

"Are you saying that Wilskie's squad car has been behind the village garage for fifty years!?" said an agog Williams.

"That's right. Vic and his partner-in-crime put it there the night of murder. I couldn't believe it when Victor told me, but I went down there after questioning him and walked to the yard behind the garage, and found the squad car covered in dirt, grime, tires flat, rusty. It clearly hasn't been touched since that day."

"Wow," said Williams, shaking his head in disbelief.

"So here's what I'm thinking. Let's say that we found Wilskie's body in the trunk of his squad car with a bullet wound to the head. We can say that Wilskie had caught men trying to break in to the factory to steal a bomb and they shot him for it."

"Will that hold up? Wouldn't there have been security guards around the factory who could say that didn't happen?"

"Well, I did some research on that and found out that all of the security guards employed at that time have been dead for many years; most of them were former cops or military, so they were quite a bit older than Vic at that time, which explains why they're all dead now."

"Sounds like we've got our official story, Chief Preston," replied Williams approvingly. "There is one more thing the Bureau would like to do for you, this Village, and Officer Wilskie: We would like to cover the cost to put on the hero's funeral that this man deserves. How does that sound?"

"That's a very nice offer, Agent Williams. Thank you," replied Preston.

As both men stood up, Williams said, "Now, I've heard that there is a nice English Pub over there at the Patriot Club. What do you say I buy you lunch?"

"The Clydesdale, great place, a lot of good memories there," replied Preston. "On the way, I'll tell you some stories about 'the Clyde,' as it's called around here, to help you appreciate it even more," said Preston as both men headed out of the office.

Chapter Nineteen
1997

Today was a day that was fifty years overdue. Today was the funeral for Officer James Wilskie. Although very few people left in the village ever met Jim Wilskie, everyone had heard the stories of the Ashbelle police officer who had simply vanished and the shameful rumors that went along with them. Fortunately, those stories were now replaced with that of a brave and courageous officer who had died in the line of duty. Preston was shocked and proud when he arrived at Far Woods Cemetery in his dress uniform and saw the size of the crowd. It was as if the entire village, who had last gathered at Chris's funeral several weeks before, had come to not only honor this brave man, but to close this dark chapter in the village's history.

A podium had been placed for Preston and others to speak. After the village president had said his part, Preston approached the podium. On his way up, he stopped to say thank you to Agent Williams in appreciation for not only paying for the funeral itself, but also for the guard that was present for the twenty-one-gun salute.

Preston had a speech prepared that he had spent most of the last few days writing, but had decided at the last minute to ditch it and just go with what was in his heart. He looked at the crowd, took a deep breath, and began to speak.

"Not often does a fifty-year old wrong get a chance to be put right, especially in such a prolific way. Officer James Wilskie, although unknown personally to most of you, was a hero. Although I was not personally around in the forties, I've been told by several of you here who were that it was a prosperous time in Ashbelle, but also a scary time. Scary not only because our young men were being sent off to the European and Pacific theaters, but also because during WWII, the Ashbelle Company had turned exclusively to making bombs for the war effort, and that made the company and the village a target to the enemy. People were proud of their part in helping the war effort, but also always had that worry of having a target over their heads. So when, on that terrible night in 1944, Officer James Wilskie laid his life on the line to stop one of those bombs from falling into what could have been enemy hands, he became a hero not only to the Village of Ashbelle, but also to the United States of America. For his unheralded bravery, he was not only ruthless murdered, but also rewarded with nasty rumors and gossip in this village over the last fifty years. I don't blame anybody, I heard the same stories about him as you all did growing up, but let us now replace those stories and rumors with the truth: that this man was a hero and an example for us all. Before the twenty-one-gun salute that is fifty years overdue, I'd like to draw your attention to the statue before you. It is of Officer James Wilskie and will forever be a reminder of his bravery and sacrifice. Thank you."

The crowd applauded as Preston walked away from the podium. After the ceremony, as Preston was walking back to his squad car, a woman came up to him and put her hand on his arm.

"Excuse me, Chief Preston. My name is Portia Jennings and James Wilskie was my father. I can't thank you enough for helping find the truth that we always knew: that he was a brave man and a loyal police officer. Shortly after my father disappeared, we moved out of the village as the rumors began to grow about him just leaving and all other sorts of nasty things. It was hard, as my mother had grown up here and loved Ashbelle.

I haven't been back since, but I look forward to stopping by and seeing Dad's grave and memorial whenever I can. My mother, God rest her soul, would have given anything to see today. Thank you from the bottom of my heart and from my entire family."

"Ma'am, I'm sorry you and your family had to go through all that. I can't imagine. I just hope we have helped heal some things here today," replied Preston.

"You have, you most definitely have. This village is blessed to have you to watch over it. Thank you again, take care, and God bless," said Portia as she walked away.

Chapter Twenty
2015

It was late Spring in Ashbelle, and the village was beautiful. The recently retired police chief, David Preston, was out for his daily walk, which took him all around the village. This was the highlight of his day, as he got to talk with residents, reminisce with them, and stay up on the latest gossip of the village.

Preston was just about to head to the cemetery like he did everyday to put a hand on Wilskie's monument when a vehicle pulled up.

"Chief Preston?" said Agent Williams as he exited the vehicle and began to walk toward Preston.

"Agent Williams, nice to see you again. How's life with the FBI these days?" asked Preston while shaking Williams' hand.

"Not bad, I'm set to retire next year, so just trying to stay in one piece," replied Williams with a smile.

"What brings you to town?" asked Preston.

"I came looking for you. I had some news I'd thought you'd like to hear."

"Okay, what's that?"

"Believe it or not, Victor died in prison last week."

"No way! He must've been one hundred years old!" replied a shocked Preston.

"Yeah, one hundred and two, actually. Can't believe he lasted that long. Anyway, that's only part of the news; the other part is even more shocking."

"Really? Let's hear it," said Preston.

"Well, Victor, unbeknownst to anyone, happened to be worth a few million dollars at his death."

"Wow," replied Preston, shocked again.

"Well, he lived like a miser, had a good job and a good pension, got his wife's life insurance when she died…lived in the same house forever, never traveled, et cetra," explained Williams.

"I suppose that makes sense."

"Well, during Victor's longer-than-expected prison term, he found God and was a completely different person at the end, apparently, than the cranky old man that he was when he went in."

"Well, that's good," replied Preston.

"Best part of the whole thing is that when he died, he left a $1.5 million scholarship fund for Ashbelle High School in Chris's name with one stipulation."

"Wow, $1.5 million! That's going to help so many kids. What was that stipulation?"

"That you, as long as you live and are able, are to be the one with the final say on where the money goes every year. He really respected you, David, at least at the end."

"Wow, I don't know what to say. That's a lot to take in."

"Well, seems like Chris will live on in this town through that gift and through you. I have to get going. Be well, my friend."

As Williams drove away, Preston waved good-bye and smiled. He took a seat on the bench next to Wilskie's memorial and thought to himself how grateful he was to have served such a great village as police chief and now how he would continue to serve it while at the same time being able to honor Chris's memory.

A few moments later, Preston got up and began to head for home; he had to tell his wife the news. As he was heading down Hill Street toward his home, he saw a couple walking in front of him.

He didn't recognize them at first, but then as they neared each other, he noticed it was Chris's mother and stepfather.

"Hello," said Preston as they all came to a stop to greet each other.

Chris' stepfather looked at Preston and said, "We had a visitor this morning, an Agent Williams from the FBI. He told us all about the scholarship set up in Chris's name by that man and about the role you are to play in it."

"Yes, I just saw Agent Williams myself and he told me all about it."

Then Chris's mom, with tears in her eyes said, "We can't think of a better person to direct the scholarship fund than you. We'll never forget everything you did when…when, well, when Chris was murdered."

"It'll be my pleasure helping keep the memory alive of such a terrific person as Chris," replied Preston, trying to stop the tears in his own eyes.

As Preston walked away toward home, he saw an Ashbelle Police car roll by. He waved at the officer. It was the newest member of the APD, Officer Adam Wilskie, grandson of Officer James Wilskie.

Preston smiled.

THE END